Nurses in the City

Finding love in a Sydney hospital…

Flatmates Grace and Lola are passionate about
their jobs as nurses at Kirribilli General Hospital.
But two hot new arrivals are about to take that
passion to a whole new level!

Grace's childhood neighbor, surgeon Marcus,
is all man now and hiding a wealth of pain.
Will Grace be the woman to heal his heart?

Lola's best friend's brother, paramedic Hamish,
is forbidden fruit. But how long can Lola fight their
fierce attraction before giving in to temptation?

Grace's Story:
Reunited with Her Brooding Surgeon
by Emily Forbes

Lola's Story:
Tempted by Mr. Off-Limits
by Amy Andrews

Available now!

Dear Reader,

A few years ago I promised Sheila Hodgson—head honcho of the Harlequin Medical Romance line— a transplant story. A bunch of time passed…

Then the opportunity arose for Emily Forbes and I to do another duo together and I suggested we use transplant medicine as the medical backdrop for the books. Having worked in intensive care units and nursed both donors and recipients in my nursing years I felt I could give my book some real authenticity and hence Lola and Hamish were born.

Lola the urban nomad and Hamish the country boy with both feet planted firmly on the ground. I do love an opposites-attract story, don't you?

I hope you enjoy reading their tug-of-love story as much as I enjoyed writing it.

Happy reading,

Love *Amy* xxx

TEMPTED BY
MR. OFF-LIMITS

———

AMY ANDREWS

HARLEQUIN® MEDICAL ROMANCE™

Recycling programs
for this product may
not exist in your area.

ISBN-13: 978-1-335-66377-1

Tempted by Mr. Off-Limits

First North American Publication 2018

Copyright © 2018 by Amy Andrews

Printed in U.S.A.

Books by Amy Andrews

Harlequin Medical Romance

Waking Up with Dr. Off-Limits
Sydney Harbor Hospital: Luca's Bad Girl
How to Mend a Broken Heart
Sydney Harbor Hospital: Evie's Bombshell
One Night She Would Never Forget
Gold Coast Angels: How to Resist Temptation
200 Harley Street: The Tortured Hero
It Happened One Night Shift
Swept Away by the Seductive Stranger
A Christmas Miracle

Visit the Author Profile page
at Harlequin.com for more titles.

I dedicate this book to my brother-in-law
Ron MacMaster, a great husband and father
who was taken too young. You are greatly missed.

**Praise for
Amy Andrews**

"Packed with humor, heart and pathos, *Swept Away
by the Seductive Stranger* is a stirring tale of second
chances, redemption and hope with a wonderfully
feisty and intelligent heroine you will adore and a
gorgeous hero whom you will love."

—*Goodreads*

CHAPTER ONE

LOLA FRASER NEEDED a drink in the worse way. Thank God for Billi's, the bar across the road from the Kirribilli General Hospital. The ice-blue neon of the welcome sign filled her with relief—she didn't think she could wait until she got home to Manly and it was less than a thirty-minute drive at nine-thirty on a Sunday night.

The place was jumping. There was some music playing on the old-fashioned jukebox but it wasn't too loud. Most of the noise was coming from a large group of people Lola recognised as belonging to the Herd Across the Harbour event. It had taken place earlier today and they were all clearly celebrating the success of the fundraising venture.

Grace, Lola's bestie and flatmate, was the renal transplant co-ordinator for the hospital and had been one of the organisers. In fact, her entire family had been heavily involved. Lola had also been roped in to help out this morning before her afternoon shift, and although she'd gratefully escaped horses, cows and, well…anything country a long time ago, there had been something magnificent about all those cattle walking over the Sydney Harbour Bridge.

Talk about a contrast—one of the world's most iconic architectural landmarks overrun by large, hooved beasts. It had certainly made a splash on news services all around the world. Not to mention the pile of money it had raised for dialysis machines for rural and remote hospitals. And then there was the exposure it had given to the Australian Organ Donor Register and the importance of talking with family about your wishes.

A conversation Lola wished her patient tonight had taken the time to have with his family. Maybe, out of his tragic death, some other families could have started living again.

And she was back to needing a drink.

She moved down the bar, away from the happy crowd. Their noise was good—celebratory and distracting—but she couldn't really relate to that right now.

Gary, a big bear of a man, took one look at her and said, 'You okay?'

Lola shook her head, a sudden rush of emotion thickening her throat. Gary had been running the bar over the road for a lot of years now and knew all the Kirribilli staff who frequented his establishment. He also knew, in that freaky bartender way, if a shift hadn't gone so well.

'Whaddya need?'

'Big, *big* glass of wine.'

He didn't bat an eyelid at her request. 'Your car in the multi-storey?'

Lola nodded. 'I'll get a cab home.' She had another afternoon shift tomorrow so she'd get a cab to work and drive her car home tomorrow night.

Within thirty seconds, Gary placed a chilled glass of white wine in front of her. It was over the standard drink line clearly marked on the glass. *Well* over.

'Let me know when you want a refill.'

Lola gave him a grateful smile. She loved it that Gary already knew this was a more-than-one-glass-of-wine night. 'Thanks.'

Raising the glass to her lips, Lola took three huge swallows and shut her eyes, trying to clear her mind of the last few hours. Working in Intensive Care was the most rewarding work she'd done in the thirty years of her life. People came to them *desperately* ill and mostly they got better and went home. And that was such an *incredible* process to be a part of.

But not everyone was so lucky.

For the most part, Lola coped with the flip side. She'd learned how to compartmentalise the tragedies and knew the importance of de-briefing with colleagues. She also knew that sometimes you weren't ready to talk about it. And for that there was booze, really loud music and streaming movies.

Sometimes sex.

And she had no problems with using any of them for their temporary amnesiac qualities.

Lola took another gulp of her wine but limited it to just the one this time.

'Now, what's a gorgeous woman like you doing sitting at a bar all by yourself?'

Lola smiled at the low voice behind her, and the fine blonde hairs at her nape that had escaped the loose low plait stood to attention. 'Hamish.'

Hamish Gibson laughed softly and easily as he plonked himself down on the chair beside her. Her heart fluttered a little as it has this morning when she'd first met him on the Harbour Bridge. He was tall and broad and good looking. And he knew it.

Patently up for some recreational sex.

But he was also Grace's brother and staying at their apartment for the night. So it would be wrong to jump his bones.

Right?

She *could* have a drink with him, though, and he wasn't exactly hard on the eyes. 'Let me buy you a drink,' she said.

He grinned that lovely easy grin she'd been so taken with this morning. She'd bet he *killed* the ladies back home with that grin. *That mouth.*

'Isn't that supposed to be my line?'

'You're in the big smoke now,' she teased. 'We Sydney women tend to be kinda forthright. Got a problem with that?'

'Absolutely none. I love forthright women.' He gestured to Gary and ordered a beer. 'And for you?'

Lola lifted her still quite full glass. 'I'm good.' She took another big swig.

Hamish's keen blue eyes narrowed a little. 'Bad shift?'

'I've had better.'

He nodded. Hamish was a paramedic so Lola was certain she didn't have to explain her current state of mind. 'You wanna talk about it?'

'Nope.' Another gulp of her wine.

'You wanna get drunk?'

'Nope. Just a little distracted.'

He grinned again and things a little lower than Lola's heart fluttered this time. 'I give good distraction.'

Lola laughed. 'You *are* good distraction.'

'And you are good for my ego, Lola Fraser.'

'Yeah. I can tell your ego is badly in need of resuscitation.'

He threw back his head and laughed and Lola followed the very masculine line of his throat etched with five o'clock shadow to a jaw so square he could have been a cartoon superhero. Was it wrong she wanted to lick him there?

Gary placed Hamish's beer on the bar in front of him and he picked it up. 'What shall we drink to?'

Lola smiled. 'Crappy shifts?'

'Here's to crappy shifts.' He tapped his glass against the rim of hers. 'And distractions.'

They were home by eleven. Lola had drunk another—standard—glass of wine and Hamish had sat on his beer. They'd chatted about the Herd Across the Harbour event and cattle and he'd made her laugh about his hometown of Toowoomba and some of the incidents he'd gone to as a paramedic. He *was* a great distraction in every sense of the word but when she'd started to yawn he'd insisted on driving them home and she'd directed.

But now they were here, Lola wasn't feeling tired. In fact, she dreaded going to bed. She wasn't drunk enough to switch off her brain—

only pleasantly buzzed—and sex with Hamish was out of the question.

Completely off-limits.

'You fancy another drink?' She headed through to the kitchen and made a beeline for the fridge. She ignored the three postcards attached with magnets to the door. They were from her Aunty May's most recent travels— India, Vietnam and South Korea. Normally they made her smile but tonight they made her feel restless.

She was off to Zimbabwe for a month next April. It couldn't come soon enough.

'Ah…sure. Okay.'

He didn't sound very sure. 'Past your bedtime?' she teased as she pulled a bottle of wine and a beer out of the fridge.

He smiled as he took the beer. His thick, wavy, nutmeg hair flopped down over his forehead and made her want to furrow her fingers in it. There were red-gold highlights in it that shone in the downlights and reminded Lola of Grace's gorgeous red hair.

'I'd have thought Grace would still be up.'

Lola snorted. 'I'm sure she is. Just not here. Did you forget she got engaged to Marcus today?'

'No.' He grinned. 'I didn't forget.'

'Yes well…' Lola poured her wine. 'I'm

pretty sure they're probably *celebrating*. If you get my drift.'

The way his gaze strayed to her mouth left Lola in no doubt he did.

'He's a good guy, yeah?'

'Oh, yeah.' Lola nodded. 'They're both hopelessly in love.'

Lola was surprised at the little pang that hit her square in the chest. She'd never yearned for a happily ever after—she liked being foot-loose and fancy-free. Why on earth would she suddenly feel like she was missing something?

She shook it away. It was just *this* night. This awful, awful night. 'Let's go out to the balcony.'

She didn't wait for him to follow her or even check to see if he was—she could *feel* the weight of his gaze on her back. On her ass, actually, and she wished she was in something more glamorous than her navy work trousers and the pale blue pinstriped blouse with the hospital logo on the left pocket.

Lola leaned against the railing when she reached her destination, looking out over the parkland opposite, the night breeze cool as befitting August in Sydney. She could just detect the faint trace of the ocean—salt and sand—despite being miles from Manly Beach.

She loved that smell and inhaled it deeply,

pulling it into her lungs, savouring it, grateful for nights like this. Grateful to be alive. And suddenly the view was blurring before her eyes and the faint echo of a thirteen-year-old girl's cries wrapped fingers around Lola's heart and squeezed.

Her patient tonight would never feel the sea breeze on his face again. His wife and two kids would probably never appreciate something as simple ever again.

'Hey.'

She hadn't heard Hamish approach and she quickly shut her eyes to stop the moisture becoming tears. But he lifted her chin with his finger and she opened them. She was conscious of the dampness on her lashes as she was drawn into his compelling blue gaze. 'Are you sure you don't want to talk about it?'

His voice was low and Lola couldn't stop staring at him. He was wearing one of those checked flannel shirts that was open at the throat and blue jeans, soft and faded from years of wear and tear. They fitted him in all the right places. He radiated warmth and smelled like beer and the salt and vinegar chips they'd eaten at the bar, and she *wanted* to talk about it.

Who knew, maybe it would help? Maybe talking with a guy who'd probably seen his fair share of his own crappy shifts would be a relief. Lola turned back to the view across the darkened park. His hand fell away, but she was conscious of his nearness, of the way his arm brushed hers.

'My patient… He was pronounced brain dead tonight. We switched him off. He had teenage kids and…' She shrugged, shivering as the echo of grief played through her mind again. 'It was…hard to watch.'

Her voice had turned husky and tears pricked again at the backs of her eyes. She blinked them away once more as he turned to his side, his hip against the railing, watching her.

'Sorry…' She dashed away a tear that had refused to be quelled. 'I'm being melodramatic.'

He shrugged. 'Some get to you more than others.'

The sentiment was simple but the level of understanding was anything but and something gave a little inside Lola at his response. There were no meaningless platitudes about *tomorrow being another day* or empty compliments about what an *angel* she must be. Hamish understood that sometimes a patient sneaked past the armour.

'True but… Just ignore me.' She shot him a watery smile.

'I'm being stupid.'

He shook his head. 'No, you're not.'

Lola gave a half laugh, half snort. 'Yes. I am. My tears aren't important.' This wasn't about her. It was about a family who'd just lost everything. 'This man's death shouldn't be about my grief. I don't know what's wrong with me tonight.'

'I think it's called being human.'

He smiled at her with such gentleness and insight she really, really wanted to cry. But she didn't, she turned blind eyes back to the view, her arm brushing his. Neither said anything for long moments as they sipped at their drinks.

'Was it trauma?' Hamish asked.

'Car accident.' Lola was glad to be switching from the *emotion* of the death to the more practical facts of it.

'Did he donate his organs?'

Hamish and Grace's sister-in-law, Merridy, had undergone a kidney transplant four years ago, so Lola knew the issue meant a lot to the Gibson family.

She shook her head. 'No.'

'Was he not a candidate?'

Lola could hear the frown in Hamish's voice as she shook her head, a lump thickening her throat. What the hell was *wrong* with her tonight? She was usually excellent at shaking this stuff off.

'He wasn't on the register?'

The lump blossomed and pressed against Lola's vocal cords. She cleared her throat. 'He was but…'

Her sentence trailed off and she could see Hamish nod in her peripheral vision as realisation dawned. It was a relief not to have to say it. That Hamish knew the cold hard facts and she didn't have to go into them or try and explain something that made no sense to most people.

'I hate when that happens.' Hamish's knuckles turned white as he gripped the railing.

'Me too.'

'It's wrong that family can override the patient in situations like that.'

She couldn't agree more but the fact of the matter was that family always had the final say in these matters, regardless of the patient's wishes.

'Why can't doctors just say, too bad, this was clearly your loved one's intention when they put their name down on the donation register?'

Lola gave a half-smile, understanding the frustration but knowing it was never as simple as that. 'Because we don't believe in further traumatising people who are already in the middle of their worst nightmare.'

It was difficult to explain how her role as a nurse changed in situations of impending death. How her duty of care shifted—mentally anyway—from her patient to the family. In a weird way they became her responsibility too and trying to help ease them through such a terrible time in their lives—even just a little—became paramount.

They were going to have to live on, after all, and how the hospital process was managed had a significant bearing on how they coped with their grief.

'Loved ones don't say no out of spite or grief or even personal belief, Hamish. They say no because they've *never* had a conversation with that person about it. And if they've never *specifically* heard that person say they want their organs donated in the event of their death. They...' Lola shrugged '...err on the side of caution.'

It was such a terrible time to have to make that kind of decision when people were grappling with so much already.

'I know, I know.' He sighed and he sounded as heavy-hearted as she'd felt when her patient's wife had tearfully declined to give consent for organ donation.

'Which is why things like Herd Across the Harbour are so important.' Lola made an effort to drag them back from the dark abyss she'd been trying to step back from all night, turning slightly to face him, the railing almost at her waist. 'Raising awareness about people having those kinds of conversations is vital. So they know and support the wishes of their nearest and dearest if it ever comes to an end-of-life situation.'

She raised her glass towards him and Hamish smiled and tapped his beer bottle against it. 'Amen.'

They didn't drink, though, they just stared at each other, the blue of his eyes as mesmerising in the night as the perfect symmetry of his jaw and cheekbones and the fullness of his mouth. They were close, their thighs almost brushing, their hands a whisper apart on the railing.

Lola was conscious of his heat and his solidness and the urge to put her head on his chest and just be held was surprisingly strong.

When was the last time she'd wanted to be just held by a man?

The need echoed in the sudden thickness of her blood and the stirring deep inside her belly, although neither of them felt particularly platonic. Confused by her feelings, she pushed up onto her tippy-toes and kissed him, trapping their drinks between them.

She shouldn't have. *She really shouldn't have.*

But, oh…it was lovely. The feel of his arms coming around her, the heat of his mouth, the swipe of his tongue. The quick rush of warmth to her breasts and belly and thighs. The funny bump of her heart in her chest.

The way he groaned her name against her mouth.

But she had to stop. 'I'm sorry.' She broke away and took a reluctant step back. 'I shouldn't have done that.'

His fingers on the railing covered hers. 'Yeah,' he whispered. 'You absolutely should have.'

Lola gave him a half-smile, touched by his certainty but knowing it couldn't go anywhere. She slipped her hand out from under his, smiled again then turned away, heading straight to her room and shutting out temptation.

CHAPTER TWO

BUT LOLA COULDN'T SLEEP. Not after finishing her glass of wine in bed or taking a bath or one of those all-natural sleeping tablets that usually did the trick. She lay awake staring at the ceiling, the events of the shift playing over and over in her head.

Her patient's wife saying, *'But there's not a scratch on him...'* and his daughter crying, *'No, Daddy!'* and his teenage son being all stoic and brave and looking so damn *stricken* it still clawed at her gut. The faces and the words turned around and around, a noisy wrenching jumble inside her head, while the oppressive weight of silence in the house practically deafened her.

She felt...alone...she realised. Damn it, she *never* felt alone. She was often here by herself overnight if Grace was at work or at Marcus's and it had never bothered her before. She'd *never* felt alone in a city. But tonight she did.

It was because Hamish was out there. She knew that. Human company—*male company*—was lying on the couch and she was in here, staring at the shadows on the ceiling. And because it wouldn't be the first time she'd turned to a man to forget a bad shift, her body was restless with confusion.

Was it healthy to *sex* away her worries? No. But it wasn't a regular habit and it sure as hell helped from time to time.

Lola had no doubt Hamish would be up for it. He'd been flirting with her from the beginning and he'd certainly been all in when she'd kissed him on the balcony. The message in his eyes when she'd pulled away had been loud and clear.

If you want to take this to the bedroom, I'm your guy.

And if he hadn't been Grace's brother, she would have followed through. And not just because she needed the distraction but because there was something about Hamish Gibson that tugged at her. She'd felt it on the bridge this morning *and* at the bar.

It was no doubt to do with his empathy, with his innate understanding of what she'd witnessed tonight. She didn't usually go for men who came from her world, particularly in these situations. Someone outside it—who didn't know or care what she'd been through—was usually a much better distraction.

Someone who only cared about getting her naked.

Who knew familiarity and empathy could be so damn sexy? Who knew they could stroke right between your legs as well as clutch at your heart?

Lola rolled on her side and stuffed her hands between her thighs to quell the heat and annoying buzz of desire. *Wasn't going to happen.* Hamish was Grace's brother. And she *couldn't* go there. No matter how much she needed the distraction. No matter how well he kissed. No matter the fire licking through her veins and roaring at the juncture of her legs.

Lola shut her eyes—tight.

Go to sleep, damn it.

At two o'clock in the morning, Lola gave up trying to fight it. Grace wasn't here—she'd texted an hour ago to say she was staying at Marcus's—and Hamish would be gone in the morning.

What could it hurt? As long as he knew it was a one-off?

Decision made, she kicked off the sheet and stood. She paused as she contemplated her attire, her underwear and a tank top. Should she dress in something else? Slip on one of her satiny scraps of lingerie that covered more but left absolutely nothing to the imagination? She'd been surprised to learn over the years that some guys preferred subtlety.

Or should she go out there buck naked?

What kind of guy was Hamish—satin and lace or bare flesh?

Oh, bloody hell. What was wrong with her? *Had she lost her freaking mind?* Hamish was probably just going to be grateful for her giving it up for him at two in the morning and smart enough to take it any way it was offered. She was going to be naked soon enough anyway.

Just get out there, Lola!

Quickly snatching a condom out of the box in her bedside drawer, she headed for her door, opened it and tiptoed down the darkened hallway. Ambient light from a variety of electrical appliances cast a faint glow into the living room and she could make out a large form on the couch. She came closer, stepping around the coffee table to avoid a collision with her shins, and the form became more defined.

He'd kicked off the sheet, which meant Lola could see a lot of bare skin—abs, legs, chest—and she looked her fill. A pair of black boxer briefs stopped her from seeing *everything* and his face was hidden by one bare arm thrown up over it. The roundness of his biceps as it pushed against his jaw was distracting as all giddy up.

As was the long stretch of his neck.

It was tempting to do something really crazy like run her fingers along that exposed, whiskery skin. Possibly her tongue.

But she needed to wake him first. She couldn't just jump on him, no matter how temptingly he was lying there.

Lola clenched her fists, the sharp foil edges of the condom cutting into her palm as she took a step towards him. Her foot landed on the only squeaky floorboard in the entire room and he was awake in an instant. She froze as his abs tensed and his body furled upwards, his legs swinging over the edge of the couch. His feet had found the floor before she had a chance to take another breath.

He blinked up at her, running his palms absently up and down the length of his bare thighs. 'Lola?'

Lola let out a shaky breath as she took a step back. 'I guess it's true what they say about country guys, then.'

'Hung like horses?' He shot her a sleepy smile. His voice was low and rumbly but alert.

She laughed and it was loud in the night. 'Light sleepers.'

'Oh, that.' He rubbed his palm along his jawline and the scratchy noise went straight to her belly button. 'Are you okay?'

Lola shook her head, her heart suddenly racing as she contemplated the width of his shoulders and the proposition she was about to lay on him. 'I...can't sleep.'

'So you came out for...a cup of warm milk?'

The smile on his face matched the one in his voice, all playful and teasing, and Lola blushed. Her cheeks actually heated! What the hell?

Since when did she start blushing?

Most nurses she knew, including herself, were generally immune to embarrassment. She'd seen far too much stuff in her job to be embarrassed by *anything*.

'No.' She held up the condom, her fingers trembling slightly, grateful for the cover of night. 'I was thinking of something more... physical.'

His gaze slid to the condom and Lola's belly clenched as he contemplated the foil packet like it was the best damn thing he'd seen all night. 'I have read,' he said after a beat or two, refocusing on her face, 'that *physical activity* is very good for promoting sleep.'

Lola's nipples puckered at the slight emphasis on 'physical activity' and she swallowed against a mouth suddenly dry as the couch fabric. 'Yeah.' She smiled. 'I read that too.'

He held out his hand. 'Come here.'

Lola's heart leapt in her chest but she ground her feet into the floor. They had to establish some ground rules. 'This can only be a one-time thing.'

'I know.'

His assurance grazed Lola's body like a physical force, rubbing against all the *good* spots, but she needed to make certain he was absolutely on the same page. 'You're leaving to-morrow,' she continued. 'We'll probably never see each other again.' This was the first time she'd met Hamish after all, despite having lived with Grace for almost all the last two years. 'And I'm good with that.'

'Me too.'

'I don't do relationships. Especially not long-distance relationships.'

He nodded again. 'I understand. We're one and done. I *am* good with it, Lola.'

'Also... I don't think we should tell Grace about this.'

He sat back a little, clearly startled at the sug-gestion, looking slightly askance. 'Do I look like I took a stupid pill to you?'

Lola laughed. He looked like he'd taken an up-for-it pill and heat wound through her ab-domen. Hamish leaned forward at the hips and crooked his finger, a small smile playing on his wicked mouth.

'Come here, *Lola.*'

The way he said her name when he was mostly naked was like fingers stroking down her belly. Lola took a small step forward, her entire body trembling with anticipation. She took another and then she was standing in front of him, the outsides of her thighs just skimming the insides of his knees.

He held his hand out and she placed the condom in his palm. He promptly shoved it under a cushion before sliding his hands onto the sides of her thighs. Lola's breath hitched as they slid all the way up and the muscles in her stomach jumped as they slid under the hem of her T-shirt, pushing it up a little.

Leaning closer, he brushed his mouth against the bare skin, his lips touching down just under her belly button. Lola's mouth parted on a soft gasp and her hands found his shoulders as their gazes locked. One hand kept travelling, pushing into the thick wavy locks of his hair, holding him there as they stared at each other, their breathing low and rough.

Then he fell back against the couch, pulling her with him, urging her legs apart so she was straddling him, the heat and pulse at her heart settling over the heat and hardness of him.

His hands slid into her hair, pulling her head down, his mouth seeking hers.

Her pulse thundered through her ears and throbbed between her legs and she moaned as their lips met. She couldn't have stopped it even had she wanted to.

And she didn't.

He swallowed it up, his mouth opening over hers, a faint trace of his toothpaste a cool undercurrent to all the heat. He kissed her slow but deep, wet and thorough, and Lola's entire body tingled and yearned as she clutched at his shoulders from her dominant position, moaning and gasping against his mouth.

He was all she could think about. His mouth and his heat and the hardness between his legs. No work, no death, no stricken children, no disbelieving wives. Just Hamish, good and hard and hot and *hers*, filling her senses and her palms and the space between her thighs.

Lola barely registered falling or the softness of landing as his hands guided her backwards. But she did register the long naked stretch of him against her. The way his hips settled into the cradle of her pelvis, the way his erection notched along the seam of her sex, the way his body pressed her hard and good into the cushions.

He was dominating her now and she loved it.

Wanted more. *Needed* more. His skin sliding over hers. His body sliding *into* hers. It was as if he could read her mind. His hands pushing her shirt up, gliding over her stomach and ribs and breasts, pulling it off over her head before returning to her breasts, squeezing and kneading, pinching her nipples, his mouth coming back hard and hot on hers, kissing and kissing and kissing until she was dizzy with the magic of his mouth, clawing at his back and gasping her pleasure.

He kissed down her neck and traced the lines of her collar bones with the tip of his tongue before lapping it over her sternum and circling her nipples, sucking each one into his mouth making her cry out, making her mutter, *'Yes, yes, yes,'* in some kind of incoherent jumble. And he kept doing it, licking and sucking as his hands pushed at her underwear and hers pushed at his until they were both free of barriers.

He broke away, tearing the foil open and rolling the condom on, then he was back and she almost lost her breath at the thickness of his erection sliding between her legs. He was big and hard, gliding through her slickness, finding her entrance and settling briefly.

'You feel so good,' he muttered, before easing inside her, slowly at first then pushing home on a groan that stirred the cells in her marrow and lit the wick on her arousal.

She flared like a torch in the night, insane with wanting him, wanting him more than she'd ever wanted anybody before, panting her need straight into his ear, '*God yes*, like that,' revelling in the thickness of him, the way he stretched her, the way he filled her. 'Just like that...'

And he gave it to her like *that* and more, rocking and pounding, kissing her again, swallowing her moans and her cries and her pants, smothering them with his own as he thrust in and pulled out, a slow steady stroke, the rhythm of his hips setting the rhythm in her blood and the sizzle in her cells. Electricity buzzed from the base of her spine to the arch of her neck.

Her mind was blank of everything but the heat and the thrust and the feel of him. The prison of his strong, rounded biceps either side of her and the broad, naked cage of his chest pinning her to the couch and the piston of his hard, narrow hips nailing her into the cushions. And the smell of him, hot and male and aroused, filling up her head, making her nostrils flare with the wild mix of toothpaste and testosterone.

Lola gasped, tearing her mouth from his as her orgasm burst around her, starting in her toes, curling them tight before rolling north, undulating through her calves and her knees and her thighs, exploding between her legs and imploding inside her belly, breaking over her in waves of ever-increasing intensity until all she could do was hold on and cry out *'Hamish!'* as it took her.

'I know.' He panted into her neck, his breathing hot and heavy, his body trembling like hers. 'I know.' He reared above her, thrusting hard one last time, his back bowed, his fists ground into the cushions either side of her head. *'Lola-a-a-a...'*

He came hard, his release bellowing out of him as his hips took over again and he rocked and rocked and rocked her, pushing her orgasm higher and higher and higher, taking her with him all the way to top until they were both spent, panting and clinging and falling back to earth in a messy heap of limbs and satisfaction.

Lola hadn't even realised she'd drifted off to sleep when Hamish moved away and she muttered something in protest. He hushed her as she drifted again. Somewhere in the drunken quagmire of her brain she thought she should get up and leave, but it was nice here in the afterglow.

Too nice to move.

Hell, a normal woman would have dragged

him back to her bed. It was bigger with a lot more potential for further nocturnal activity of the carnal kind. But then he was back and he was shuffling in behind her, his heavy arm dragging her close as he spooned her and she could barely open her eyes let alone co-ordinate her brain and limbs to make a move.

She was finally in a place where there was *nothing* on her mind and she liked it there.

She liked it very, very much.

CHAPTER THREE

Three months later...

HAMISH WASN'T SURE how he was going to be
greeted by Lola as he stood in front of her door.
Sure, they'd *spoken* in the last few weeks since
Grace had arranged for him to live with Lola
for the next two months while he did his urban
intensive care rotation, but they hadn't *seen*
each other since that night.

And he still wasn't sure this was the wis-
est idea.

He'd assured Lola that he could find somewhere else. Had stressed that she shouldn't let
Grace steamroller her into sharing her home
with him because his sister felt guilty about
her snap decision to finally move in with Marcus. It was true, someone paying the rent for
the next eight weeks would give Lola time and
breathing space to find the *right* roomie rather

than just *a* roomie, but Grace wasn't aware of their history.

Unless Lola had told Grace. But he didn't think his sister would be so keen on this proposed temporary arrangement if that had been the case. Neither did he think for a single second that he wouldn't have heard from her about it if she did know.

Lola had assured him she hadn't felt backed into a corner and it made perfect sense for him to live with her temporarily. It would help her out and their apartment was conveniently located for him.

Perfect sense.

Except for their chemistry. And for the number of times he'd thought about her these past three months. He'd told her it had been unforgettable and that had proved to be frustratingly true. How often had he thought about ringing her? Or sending her flirty texts? Not to mention how often he'd dreamed about her.

About what they'd done. And the things he still wanted to do.

Things that woke him in the middle of the night with her scent in his nostrils and a raging erection that never seemed satisfied with his hand. He shut his eyes against the movie reel of images.

Just roomies.

That's what she'd insisted on when they'd spoken about the possibility of this. Insisted that what had happened between them was in the past and they weren't going to speak of it again. They definitely weren't going to *act* on it again.

Just roomies. That was the deal-breaker, she'd said.

And he'd agreed. After all, it hadn't seemed *too* difficult over a thousand kilometres away. But standing in front of her door like this, the *reality* of her looming, was an entirely different prospect. He felt like a nervous teenager, which was utterly idiotic.

Where was the country guy who could rope a cow, ride a horse, mend a fence and fix just about any engine? Where was the paramedic who could do CPR for an hour, stabilise a trauma victim in the middle of nowhere in the pouring rain, smash a window or rip off a door and insert an IV practically hanging upside down like a bat in the shell of car crashed halfway down a mountain?

That's who he was. So he *could* share a home, in a purely platonic way, with a woman he was hot for.

Because he was a grown man, damn it!

Hamish knocked quickly before he stood any longer staring at the door like he'd lost his mind. His hand shook and his pulse spiked as the sound of her footsteps drew nearer.

The door opened abruptly and Lola stood there in her uniform. He wondered absently if she was going *to* or coming *from* work as his body registered more basic details. Like her gorgeous green eyes and the blonde curls pulled back into a loose plait at her nape, just as it had been that night at Billi's.

Suddenly he was back there again, remembering how much she'd *touched* him that night. *Emotionally.* How much he'd wanted to comfort her. To ease the burden so clearly weighing heavily on her shoulders.

To make her smile.

She smiled at him now and he blinked and came back to the present. It was the kind of smile she'd given him when she'd first met him on the harbour bridge that morning—friendly and open. The kind of smile reserved for a best friend's brother or a new roomie. Like they were buddies. *Mates.*

Like he'd never been inside her body.

She'd obviously put what had happened between them behind her. Way, *way* behind her.

'Hey, you.' She leaned forward, rising on tiptoe to kiss him on the cheek.

Like a sister.

It was such an exaggeratedly platonic kiss

but his body tensed in recognition anyway. She was soft and warm and smelled exactly like he remembered, and he fought the urge to turn his head and kiss her properly.

She pulled back and smiled another friendly smile and he forced himself to relax. Forced himself to lounge lazily in the doorway and pretend he didn't want to be inside her again. *Right now.* Because he really, really did.

This is what you agreed to, *dumbass.*

'That all you got?' She tipped her chin at his battered-looking duffel bag.

Hamish glanced down, pleased to have some other direction to look. 'Should I have more?' She didn't seem impressed by his ninja packing skills.

She tutted and shook her head. 'After two months in the city you'll need that for your skin products alone.'

Laughter danced in her eyes and Hamish was impressed with her ability to act like nothing had happened between them while he felt stripped bare. Lola Fraser was as cool as a cucumber.

'I'll have you all metrosexual before you know it.'

Hamish laughed. Was that what she liked in a man? A guy who spent more time in front of the mirror than she did? Who used skin care products and waxed places that he wouldn't let hot wax anywhere near? 'Thanks. I'm happy with the way I am.'

And so were you. He suppressed the urge to give voice to the thought. He wasn't naive enough to think he'd been anything other than a port in a storm for Lola. A convenient distraction. He'd known full well what he'd been agreeing to that night.

Hell, he'd been *more* than happy to be used.

'Ah I see. You can take the boy out of the country—'

'But not the country out of the boy.' He laughed again as he finished the saying.

She grinned and said, 'We'll see,' then stood aside. 'Come on in.'

Hamish picked up his duffel bag and followed her inside. Lola gave him a quick tour even though he was familiar with the layout from that night three months ago and nothing appeared to have changed.

The couch was *definitely* the same. He had no idea how he was going to sit on it with her without some seriously sexy flashbacks.

'And this is Grace's room.' Lola walked past a shut door on the opposite side of the short hallway, which Hamish assumed was Lola's room. 'She moved out a couple of days ago.'

Hamish hadn't been in his sister's bedroom

when he'd last been here. He hadn't been in Lola's either. Not that that had stopped them…

'Make yourself at home.' She swept her arm around to indicate the space. 'It's a good size with big built-in cupboards and several power points if you want a TV or something in here.'

Hamish looked around. Grace had left her bed for him and the bedside tables. Everything was ruthlessly clean as per his sister's ways. They could have taken an appendix out on the stripped mattress. Although now they were both in the room together with a massive bed dominating the space, other things they could do on the mattress came to mind.

Lola was staring at it too as if she was just realising the level of temptation it represented. 'There are sheets, pillows, blankets, etcetera in the linen cupboard in the hallway.'

'Thanks.' Hamish threw his bag on the bed to fill up the acres of space staring back at them. And to stop himself from throwing her on it instead.

The action seemed to snap Lola out of her fixation. 'And that's it.' She turned. 'Tour over.'

Once again Hamish followed her down the hallway and into the kitchen, where she grabbed her bag and keys off the counter top. 'I'm sorry, I have to run now or I'll be late for work. I couldn't swap the shift.'

She didn't sound that sorry. In fact, she was jingling the keys like she couldn't wait to get out of there.

'It's fine.'

A part of him had assumed she'd be home this weekend to help him get settled. *Which was ridiculous.* He was a thirty-year-old man living in one of the world's most exciting cities—he didn't need to have his hand held.

And Lola was a shift worker, just like him. With bills to pay and a twenty-four-hour roster she helped to fill, including Saturdays. She had her own life that didn't involve pandering to her friend's brother.

'I'm sure I can occupy myself. What time do you finish?'

She fished in her bag and pulled out her sunglasses, opening the arms and perching them on the top of her head. 'I'm on till nine-thirty tonight. I should be home by ten, providing everything is calm at work.'

'Cool.'

'Help yourself to whatever's in the fridge. There's a supermarket three blocks away, if you're looking for something in particular. Grace and I usually shopped together and split the bill but we can discuss those details tomorrow.'

Hamish nodded. 'I'm having dinner with

Grace and Marcus tonight actually. At their new apartment. So we'll probably be getting in around the same time.'

'Oh…right.' She glanced away and Hamish wondered if she was remembering the last time they'd been here together at night. She had some colour in her cheeks when her gaze met his again. 'Don't feel like you have to be home for me. If you want to have a few drinks and end up crashing at theirs, that's fine. I'm often here by myself, it doesn't bother me.'

Hamish didn't think anything much bothered Lola. There was a streak of independence about her that grabbed him by his country-boy balls. But *he* knew that under all that Independent Woman of the World crust was someone who could break like a little girl and he really hoped she didn't feel the need to pretend to be tough all the time to compensate for how vulnerable she'd been the last time they'd met.

That would be an exhausting eight weeks for her.

And he just wanted Lola to be Lola. He could handle whatever she threw at him.

'And miss my first night in my new home?' He smiled at her to keep it light. 'No way.'

'Okay, well…' She nodded. 'I'll…see you later.'

She turned and walked away, choosing the

longer route rather than brush past him—
interesting—and within seconds he was listening to the quiet click of the front door as it shut.

Well…that was an anti-climax. He'd been
building this meeting up in his head for weeks.
None of the scenarios had involved Lola bolt-
ing within twenty minutes of his arrival. Still, it
had been good, seeing her again. And she had
definitely avoided any chance that they might
come into contact as she'd left.

That had to mean something, right?

Hamish rolled his eyes as he realised where
his brain was heading. *Get a grip,* idiot. *Not
going to happen.*

And he went to unpack and make up his bed.

It was a relief to get to work. A relief to stop
thinking about Hamish. It was crazy but Lola
hadn't expected to feel what she'd felt when
she'd opened the door to him. She'd actually
been looking forward to seeing Hamish again.
Quite aside from the sex, he was a nice guy and
a fun to be around. Even a few months later she
still caught herself smiling at the memory of
the note she'd found the morning after they'd
had sex on the couch.

*You looked so beautiful sleeping I didn't
want to disturb you.*

I'm heading home now.
Thank you for an unforgettable night.
Hamish

He'd drawn a smiley face beside his name and Lola had laughed and hugged it to her chest, secretly thrilled to be *unforgettable*.

Sure, she'd known their first meeting after that night would be awkward to begin with but had expected it to dissipate quickly.

She'd been dead wrong about that.

His presence on her doorstep—big and solid, more jaw than any man had a right to—had been like a shockwave breaking over her. She'd felt like she was having some kind of out-of-body experience, where she was above herself, looking down, the universe whispering *He's the one* in her ear.

She'd panicked. Hell, she was *still* panicking.

Firstly, she didn't believe in *the one*. Sure, she knew people stayed together for ever. Her parents had been married for thirty-two years. But to her it was absurd to think there was only *one* person out there for everyone. It was more statistically believable, given the entire population of the world, that there were many *ones* out there.

People just didn't know it because they were too busy with their current *one*.

Secondly, she honestly believed finding *the one* didn't apply to every person on the planet. Lola believed some people were destined to never settle down, that they were too content with the company of many and being children of the world to ground themselves.

And that was the category into which Lola fell. Into which Great-Aunt May fell. A spinster at seventy-five, May hadn't needed *the one* to be fulfilled. Lola had never known a person more accomplished, more well travelled or more Zen with her life.

And, thirdly, if Lola fell and smacked her head and had a complete personality change and suddenly *did* believe in such nonsense, her *one* would never be a guy from a small town.

Never.

She'd run from a small town for a reason. She hadn't wanted to be with a guy who was content to stay put, whose whole life was his patch of dirt or his business, or the place he'd grown up. Which was why her reaction to Hamish was so disconcerting.

Hamish Gibson *couldn't* be the one for her.

No. She was just really…sexually attracted to him. Hell, she'd thought about him so much these past three months it was only natural to have had a reaction to him when she'd opened the door and seen him standing right in front of her.

But she wasn't going there again.

Which was why work was such a blessing. Something else to occupy her brain. And, *yowsers*, did she need it today to deal with her critical patient.

Emma Green was twenty-three years old and in acute cardiac failure. She'd been born with a complex cardiac disorder and had endured several operations and bucketloads of medication already in her young life. But a mild illness had pushed her system to the limit and her enlarged heart muscle into the danger zone.

She'd gone into cardiac arrest at the start of the shift down in the emergency department and had been brought to ICU in a critical condition. Which meant it was a whirlwind of a shift. There were a lot of drugs to give, bloods to take, tests to run. Medication and ventilation settings were constantly tweaked and adjusted as the intensive care team responded to Emma's condition minute by minute.

As well as that, there was a veritable royal flush of specialists and their entourages constantly in and out, needing extra things, sucking up time she didn't have, all wanting their orders prioritised. There were cardiac and respiratory teams as well as radiologists and pharmacists, physiotherapists and social workers.

And there was Emma's family to deal with. Her parents, who had already been through so much with Emma over the years. Her mother teary, her father stoic—both old hands at the jargon and the solemn medical faces. And Emma's boyfriend, Barry, who was not. He was an emotional wreck, swinging from sad to angry, from positive to despondent.

Not that she could blame him. Emma looked awful. There was barely a spare inch of skin that wasn't criss-crossed by some kind of tubing or wires. She had a huge tube in her nose where the life support was connected and securing it obscured half of her face, which was puffy—as was the rest of her body—from days of retained fluid due to her worsening cardiac condition.

Lola was used to this environment, to how terrible critical patients could look. She was immune to it. But she understood full well how hard it was for people to see someone they loved in this condition. She'd witnessed the shocked gasps too many times, the audible sobs as the sucker-punch landed.

The gravity of the situation always landed with a blow. The sudden knowledge that their loved one was really, *really* sick, that they could die, was a terrible whammy. So Emma's boy-friend's reactions were perfectly normal, as far as Lola was concerned.

And all just part of her job.

'It really is okay to talk to her,' Lola assured Barry as he sat rigidly in a chair by the window, repeatedly finger-combing his hair. It was the first time he'd been alone with Emma since she'd been admitted. Her mother and father were taking it in turns to sit with Barry at the bedside but they'd both ducked out for a much-needed cup of coffee and a bite to eat.

Barry glanced at Emma and shook his head. 'I don't want to get in the way or bump anything.'

Lola smiled. 'It's okay, I'll be right here keeping an eye on you.' She kept it light because she could tell that Barry was petrified of the high-tech environment, which was quite common. 'And I promise I'll push you out the way if I need to, okay?'

He gave a worried laugh, still obviously doubtful, and Lola nodded encouragingly and smiled again. 'I'm sure she'd love to hear your voice.'

His eyes flew to Lola's in alarm. 'I thought she was sedated.'

'She is,' Lola replied calmly. 'But even un-conscious patients can still hear things. There have been plenty of people who've woken from comas or sedation and been able to recite bedside conversations word for word.'

Barry chewed on his bottom lip. 'I…don't know what to say to her.'

The despair in his voice hit Lola in every way. Barry was clearly overwhelmed by everything. She gestured him over to the seat Emma's mother had vacated not that long ago. He came reluctantly.

'Just tell her you're here,' Lola said, as he sat. 'Tell her you love her. Tell her she's in safe hands.'

'Okay.' Barry's voice trembled a little.

Lola turned to her patient. 'Emma,' she said quietly, placing a gentle hand on Emma's forearm, 'Barry's here. He's going to sit with you for a while.'

There wasn't any response from Emma— Lola didn't expect there would be—just the steady rise and fall of her chest and the rapid blipping of her monitor. Lola smiled at Barry as she withdrew her hand. 'Just put your hand where I had mine, okay? There's nothing you can bump there.' Barry tentatively slid his hand into place and Lola nodded. 'That's good. Now just talk to her.'

Lola moved away but not very far, hovering until Barry became more confident. He didn't say anything for a moment or two and when he started his voice was shaky but he *started*. 'Hey, Emsy.' His voice cracked and he cleared it. 'I'm here and… I'm not going anywhere. You're in good hands and everything's going to be okay.'

Lola wasn't entirely sure that was true. She knew how fragile Emma's condition was and part of her was truly worried her patient wasn't going to make it through the shift. But humans needed hope to go on, to *endure*, and she'd certainly been proved wrong before by patients.

Barry was doing the right thing. For him *and* for Emma.

CHAPTER FOUR

'So? When *are* you going to settle down?'

Hamish sighed at his sister, who was slightly tipsy after a few glasses of champagne. They were sitting on the balcony of their new apartment, which was also in Manly but at the more exclusive end, with harbour views. Marcus had moved out of his apartment near Kirribilli General when he and Grace had decided to move in together because they'd wanted an apartment that was *theirs*.

'God, you're like a reformed smoker. You're in love so you want everyone else to be as well.'

Grace smiled at Marcus, who smiled back as he slid his hand onto her nape. Hamish rolled his eyes at them but it was obvious his sister was in love and he was happy for her. She'd had a tough time in her first serious relationship so it was good to see her like this.

'You're thirty, Hamish. You're not getting

any younger. Surely there has to be some girl in Toowoomba who takes your fancy.'

'There's no point getting into a relationship when I'm hoping to spend a few years doing rural service after the course is done.'

Hamish had recently been passed over for a transfer to a station in the far west of the state because he didn't have an official intensive care paramedic qualification, even though he had the skills. It had spurred him to apply for a position on the course.

'It's hardly fair to get involved with someone knowing I could be off to the back of beyond at a moment's notice,' he added.

Grace sighed in exasperation. 'Maybe she'd want to go with you.'

Unbidden, an image of Lola slipped into his mind. He couldn't begin to imagine her in a small country town. She'd cornered the market in exotic city girl. She was like a hothouse flower—temperamental, high maintenance— and the outback was no place for hothouse flowers.

Women had to be more like forage sorghum. Durable and tough. And although Lola *was* tough and independent in many ways, there was something indefinably *urban* about her.

'I don't know whether you know this or not, but you're a bit of catch, Hamish Gibson. Good looking even, though it pains me to admit it. Don't you think so, Marcus?'

Grace smiled at her fiancé, a teasing light in her eyes. 'Absolutely,' he agreed, his expression totally deadpan. 'I was just saying that very thing to Lola the other day.'

Lola.

It seemed the universe was doing its best to keep her on his mind. 'And did she agree?' Hamish was pretty sure Marcus was just making it up to indulge his sister but, hell, if they'd had a conversation about him, then Hamish wanted to know!

'Of course she'd agree,' Grace said immediately. 'Lola can pick good looking out of a Sydney New Year's Eve crowd blindfolded.'

Hamish grinned at his sister. 'I'll have to remember that this New Year.'

Something in Hamish's voice must have pinged on his sister's radar. Apparently she wasn't tipsy *enough* to dull that sucker. Her eyes narrowed as her gaze zeroed in on him. '*No*, Hamish.'

'What?' Hamish spread his hands in an innocent gesture.

'You and Lola would *not* be good for each other.'

Hamish grabbed his chest as if she'd wounded him. 'Why not?'

'Because you're too alike. You're both flirts. You like the conquest but suck at any follow-through. You have to *live together* for two months, Hamish. That's a lot of awkward break-fasts. And I don't want to be caught in the mid-dle between you two or have my friendship with Lola jeopardised because you couldn't keep it in your pants.'

Hamish didn't think Lola would be the one who'd get burned in a relationship between the two of them. He at least was open to the idea of relationships—she, on the other hand, was not. He glanced at his soon-to-be brother-in-law. 'Help me out here, man.'

Marcus laughed and shook his head. 'You're on your own, buddy.'

'C'mon, dude. Solidarity.'

Grace shook her head at her brother. 'In an hour I'm going to take my fiancé to bed and do bad things to him. You think he's going to side with you?'

Hamish glanced at a clearly besotted Mar-cus, who was smiling at Grace like the sun rose and set with her, and a wave of hot green jealousy swamped his chest. He wanted that. What his sister had found with Marcus.

Contrary to *apparent* popular opinion, he'd never been opposed to settling down. He just hadn't found the right woman. For ever was, after all, a *long* time! But watching these two together…

They were the perfect advertisement for happily ever after.

Once upon a time the idea of eternal monogamy would have sent him running for the hills but these two sure knew how to sell it.

'Okay. Well, that was TMI.' He gave the lovebirds an exaggerated grimace. 'And is definitely my cue to go.'

He stood, but his sister wasn't done with him yet. 'I mean it, Hamish. I wouldn't have suggested you move in with Lola if I thought you'd make a move on her.'

'I'm not going to,' he protested.

Clearly, Grace didn't believe him. 'She's off-limits, okay?'

He was much too much of a gentleman to suggest Grace have this conversation with her bestie who had all but jumped him three months ago. But it did annoy him that somehow he was the bad guy here. 'I think Lola can take care of herself.'

Grace shook her head at his statement, thankfully a little too tipsy to read anything into his terseness. 'She comes across that way, I know. Brash and tough and in control. But she feels things as deeply as the next woman.'

A memory of Lola's glistening eyelashes

flashed on his retinas, the weight of her sadness about her patient as tangible now as it had been that night. Hamish sighed. Yeah. He knew how deeply Lola felt.

'Lola and I are roomies *only*.' He moved around to his sister and kissed her on the top of her head. 'Thank you for dinner.' She went to stand but he placed a hand on her shoulder. 'You guys stay there. I can let myself out.'

Grace squeezed the hand on her shoulder. 'Good luck on Monday. Ring me and let me know how your first shift went.'

'I will.' Hamish shook Marcus's hand. 'Goodnight.'

He left them to it, happy that his sister had found love but pleased to be away from their enviable public displays of affection.

Lola enjoyed about five seconds of contentment when she woke on Sunday morning before she remembered who was sleeping in the room across the hallway.

The feeling evaporated immediately.

She rolled her head to the side. Nine thirty. Normally she'd stretch and sigh happily and contemplate a lazy Sunday morning. No work to get to. No place to be. Her time her own.

Normally she'd walk down to one of the cafés that lined the Manly esplanade to eat smashed avocado and feta on rye bread while she watched people amble past. Maybe even stay in bed, read a good book. Or sloth around in front of the television, watching rom coms and eating Vegemite toast.

But she wasn't going to be able to sloth around for the next two months. Because Hamish was here.

Lola stared at the ceiling fan turning lazy circles above her. It was dark and cool in her room as it was on the western side of the apartment but the prediction was for a warm day. She strained her ears to hear any movement from outside.

Was he up?

Lola shut her eyes as that led to completely inappropriate thoughts and a strange dropping sensation in the pit of her stomach.

Do not think about Hamish being *up,* Lola.

Was he out of bed? That was more appropriate. She couldn't hear any noises but she'd bet her last cent he was. He was a country boy after all. And she'd known enough of them in her life to know they liked their sunrises.

Ugh. Give her a sunset any day.

Gathering her courage, she sat up and swung her legs out of bed. She had to face him some time. She couldn't spend the next two months avoiding him like she had yesterday, running out on him about twenty minutes after he'd arrived and nodding a quick hello to him last night before heading to her room with the excuse of being tired.

So just get out there, already, and face him!

Dressing quickly in a simple floral sundress with shoestring straps, Lola pulled the band on her plait and fluffed out her hair a little. She'd left it in overnight to help with knot control and to tame the curls to a crinkly wave instead of a springy mess.

But that was it—she refused to make herself pretty for Hamish. Normally when meeting a guy she'd put on some make-up, spray on her favourite perfume and wear her best lingerie. Today she was wearing no make-up, she smelled only of the washing powder she used on her clothes and she deliberately chose mismatched, *comfortable* underwear.

Not that he was in the kitchen or the living room when she made an appearance and, for a second, a ribbon of hope wound through her belly before she flicked her gaze to the balcony to find him sitting at the table. Resigned, Lola poured two glasses of juice, slamming most of hers down before topping it up and wondering if it was too early for a slug of vodka.

Pulling in a steadying breath, she picked up the glasses and went out to make polite conversation. He turned as she slid the screen door open. Her heart was practically in her mouth as she prepared herself for her body to go crazy again but the incredibly visceral reaction from yesterday didn't reappear and Lola smiled in relief.

It had clearly been an anomaly.

He smiled back and her belly swooped but it was still an improvement on yesterday. Plus, he *was* sitting there shirtless. A damp pair of running shorts clinging to his thighs was the only thing keeping him decent and that was up for debate.

'You've been for a run?' Lola gave herself full marks for how normal she sounded as she slid his glass across the tabletop. She was going to need to channel a lot of that if he was planning on walking around here shirtless very often.

'Yep.' He lifted the glass as if he was toasting her and swallowed the whole thing in several long gulps. Gulps that drew her gaze to the stretch of his neck and those gingery whiskers. 'Thanks.' He put the glass on the table. 'I needed that.'

She noticed he had an empty water bottle by his elbow.

'I can get you some more.' Lola stood. She needed a moment after that display of manliness. Escaping to the fridge seemed the perfect excuse.

He waved her back down. 'Nah. I'm good.'

'So you…run every morning.'

'Not every morning. But regularly enough. I figured it was a good way to get to know the neighbourhood.'

'Did you make it to the beach?'

'Yep. Ran along the esplanade. It's very different to the scenery I'm used to.'

It was about five kilometres to the beach so he'd already run ten kilometres this morning. *While she was sleeping.* She'd have felt like a sloth if she was capable of feeling anything other than lust.

'A lot more beach, I'd imagine.' Toowoomba was a regional inland city, well over a hundred kilometres to the nearest beach.

'Yes.' He laughed. 'Are you a runner?'

It was Lola's turn to laugh. 'I'm more of a hit-and-miss yoga in the park kinda gal.' If she was going to get hot, sweaty and breathless, she could think of much more satisfying ways to do it. Preferably naked.

'I saw a group doing that.'

'Yeah, there's a regular morning and afternoon class not far from the beach.'

Lola hadn't been in a while. Who knew, maybe living with Mr Exercise would guilt her into being more energetic herself and she was clearly going to need to put her sexual energy somewhere. Just sitting opposite him was hell on her libido.

'What are your plans for the day?' Time to move the conversation to safer territory.

He shrugged those big bare shoulders and Lola resisted the urge to stare. 'Thought I'd do a bit of sightseeing. It's pretty full on for the next couple of weeks. Might take me a while to get out again.'

'That's a great idea. It's not your first time to Sydney, though?'

'No. I've been a few times but until recently not for almost ten years.'

Lola only just stopped herself from gaping at Hamish. Ten years? Had he been *anywhere* in a decade? 'So you'll be doing the usual, then? You saw the bridge a few months ago, probably more intimately than anyone in the city, actually. You should definitely climb it while you're here.'

Lola had climbed the Sydney Harbour Bridge several times. She loved the rush of adrenaline that heights gave her. That any kind of precarious situation gave her—from white-water rafting to bungee jumping to zip lining.

The thrill. The buzz. It was better than sex. It was also why she was such a good ICU nurse. She knew how to ride the adrenaline in critical situations. She appreciated how it honed her reactions and sharpened her focus. She thrived on how well she anticipated orders, knowing what was going to be asked for even before it was, putting her hand to something a second before the doctor wanted it.

'I'd love to climb it. It's on my to-do list. Today I was just going to get a ferry across to Circular Quay and check out the Opera House and Darling Harbour.'

Lola glanced at the layers of blue sky crowning the ancient trees in the park opposite, pleased for the distraction from his body. 'It's a good day for it. And an easy walk into the city from there.'

Especially for someone who'd just run ten kilometres. And had those legs. And those abs. And that chest.

Bloody hell.

'Grace's favourite haunt is the Rocks area; you'll find a lot of old convict-era stuff there. You can walk it or jump on one of those hop-on, hop-off buses.'

'And what's *your* favourite haunt?'

Lola's breath caught at the tease in his tone and the flirt in his smile. 'Sydney's such a beautiful city, it's hard to choose.'

'Oh, come on.' He rolled his eyes at her.

'You must have a place you love more than any other.'

She did. But… 'My favourite place is not a tourist spot.'

'Ah. It's a secret? Even better.'

Lola smiled at him—she couldn't not. He was hard to resist when he was teasing, so endearingly boyish. He must have broken some hearts in high school.

'Not a secret. It's just a street I really love.'

'Does this street have a name? Spill, woman.'

Lola laughed. This was better. If she could hide behind some friendly teasing and banter the next couple of months might not be so awkward. 'I find these things are more meaningful if you stumble across them yourself.'

He snorted. 'I'm here for two months. How long did it take you to find it?'

She smiled. 'About two years.'

'Well, then.' He stood and Lola's pulse fluttered. 'I insist you take me there. Today. And I solemnly swear…' he slapped a clenched fist against his sternum, which was dizzily distracting '…to keep it a secret, on pain of death.'

Lola hadn't shown anyone her spot. Well, she'd told Grace and May about it but neither of them had seen it yet and she'd never really wanted to share it with a guy. She couldn't have borne it if he'd been dismissive of something that was essentially girly.

But, surprisingly, she *wanted* to show Hamish. Maybe she was being influenced by the whole country-boy thing but she had a feeling he appreciated nature and that he'd understand why she loved it so much.

And she hadn't checked it out this season yet so what better way to visit than playing tour guide? Plus it would occupy the day and give them a chance to establish a rapport that wasn't sexual. After today they'd probably pass like ships in the night—the hazards of shift work—so starting as she meant them to go on was a good idea.

'Okay.' She nodded. 'But only because this is actually the most perfect time of year to see it.'

'Well, that sounds even more intriguing. I'll just have a quick shower. Give me fifteen minutes.'

Lola's gaze followed him into the apartment. Broad shoulders swept down to a pair of fascinating dimples just above the waistband of his shorts. Two tight ass cheeks filling out said shorts in a way that almost made Lola believe in miracles.

And possibilities.

She tried really hard not to imagine him stripping off and stepping into the shower, water clinging to his body, running *everywhere*, wet and soapy and slippery.

She failed dramatically.

CHAPTER FIVE

WITHIN HALF AN hour Hamish was following Lola onto one of the harbour's iconic yellow and green ferries, enjoying the way her sundress fluttered around mid-thigh and the way she kept scooping up her right shoulder strap as it slipped off repeatedly.

He was pleased but surprised she'd agreed to this outing. He'd been expecting to be rebuffed, for her to keep putting him firmly at a distance. But then she'd invited him to her secret spot as if she'd made some kind of decision to accept him and their situation and wild horses couldn't have dragged him away.

He liked Lola and, who knew, maybe they could even become friends? He doubted they were the only two people in the world who'd fallen into bed and wound up as friends.

'So, we're taking the ferry?' Hamish said as Lola led him to the bow and lowered herself into one of the open-air seats. She looked very city chic in her big sunglasses, short and cute and curvy, her hair blowing around her shoulders, her cutesy dress riding up high on her thighs.

Hamish felt very *country* next to her.

'Yep. Have you been on the harbour before?'

He nodded. 'When I was in high school. Mum and Dad took us on the ferry to Taronga Zoo.'

The engines rumbled out of idle and the boat pulled away from the wharf. She breathed in deeply and sighed. 'I love taking the ferry. We're so lucky here, the harbour is gorgeous. The best in the world.'

Hamish laughed. 'Biased much?' It *was* a beautiful day, though. The sky was a stark blue dome unblemished by clouds, the sun a glorious shining bauble, refracting its golden-white light across the surface of the water like a glitter ball.

'Nope.' She shook her head and her curls, already fluttering in the breeze, swung some more. 'Trust me, I've been to a lot of harbours but Sydney wins the prize.'

'Well travelled, huh?'

Hamish realised he didn't know much about Lola at all. And the only person he could ask was his sister, who would have been highly suspicious of his interest.

'I've done quite a bit of travelling, yes.'

'What's quite a bit?'

She crossed one leg over the other and Hamish tried not to look at the dress hem riding up a little more. 'I lived in the UK for several years after I finished my degree. I did a lot of agency nursing to support my travel obsession. I've been back here for four years but go travelling again at least once a year. I've backpacked extensively through Asia, Europe and America and seen a little of Africa.'

Hamish whistled. 'Intrepid. I like it. Got any favourites?'

She didn't hesitate. 'India. It's such a land of contrasts. And Iceland. So majestic.' She glanced at him and he could just make out her eyes behind those dark brown lenses. 'It's my goal to go to every country in the world before I die.'

'A worthy goal.'

'I'm off to Zimbabwe next April.'

'On a safari thing?'

She smiled. 'For some of it. What about you? Ever had a hankering to see the world or are you one of those people who think living in the country is the be all and end all?'

Hamish blinked at the fine seam of bitterness entrenched in her words. 'Hey,' he protested, keeping it light. 'What have you got against living in the country? Don't knock it till you've tried it.'

She snorted and even that was cute. 'No, thanks. I spent seventeen years in the middle of bloody nowhere. I've paid my dues.'

Hamish stared at her. Lola Fraser had come from the sticks? He'd never met a female more *urban* in his life. 'Whereabouts?'

'You won't have heard of it.'

Hamish folded his arms. 'Try me.'

He was pretty sure she was rolling her eyes at him behind those shades.

'Doongabi.'

Yeah…she was right. He hadn't heard of it. 'Nope.'

'Imagine my surprise.' He could *hear* the eye-roll now. 'It's a rural community way past west of Dubbo, population two thousand.'

'And you couldn't wait to get out?'

'You can say that again.'

'Was it that bad?' Hamish was intrigued now.

She sighed. 'No.' Her strap slipped down giving him a peek at the slope of her breast before she pulled it back into place. 'It's a nice enough town, if that's your thing, I suppose. But it's hard to be put in a small-town strait-jacket when you were born a free spirit.'

'So you're a gypsy, huh?'

Physically she was far from the traditional gypsy type—she was blonde and busty rather than exotic and reedy—but he supposed *gypsy* was a state of mind.

'Yes. I am.' The ferry horn tooted almost directly above their heads. 'Always have been. I'm a living-in-the-moment kinda woman, although I suspect...' A smile touched her mouth. 'You probably already know that.'

Hamish acknowledged her reference with a slight smile of his own and she continued, 'I've always craved adventure. I wanted to bungee jump and climb mountains and parasail and deep sea dive and jump out of planes.'

He nodded. 'And you can't do any of that in Doongabi.'

She laughed and Hamish felt it all the way down to his toes before the breeze snatched it away. 'No.'

'Have you ever gone back?'

'I've been back a few times. For Christmas.'

'Are your parents still alive? Don't you miss them?'

'Yes. They're both still on the farm.'

The farm? Try as he might, Hamish couldn't believe Lola had come from a farming background. She was as at home in Sydney as the sails of the Opera House.

'And, yes, I do miss them in the way you

miss people you love when you haven't seen them for a long time. But they don't really *get* me and I think it's honestly as much a relief for them as it is for me when I head back to Sydney.'

'Why don't they *get* you?' Hamish felt sorry for Lola. Sure, his family had their disagreements and their differences but he'd always felt like he belonged. Like his parents *got* him.

She glanced away, the back of her head resting on the wall behind. 'Doongabi's the kind of place that people tie themselves to. Generations of families, including my father's and my mother's, have come from the district. And that's fine.' She rolled her head to look at him, the frown crinkling her forehead speaking of her turmoil. 'It's their lives and it's their choice. But…how can it be a choice?'

Her eyebrows raised in question but Hamish was sure the question was rhetorical.

'They don't *know* anything else. Women… tie themselves there to Doongabi men and have Doongabi babies, without ever venturing out into the world to see what else is on offer. They're so stuck in their ways. Unwilling to change a century of this-is-the-way-we-do-it-here.'

She sighed heavily and, once again, Hamish

felt for Lola. She obviously grappled with her mixed feelings.

'And I…wanted to fly. So…' She shrugged. 'My mother blames her aunt.'

'Her aunt?'

'My Great-Aunt May.'

'Oh…the postcards on the fridge.' She smiled at him then and it was so big and genuine it almost stole Hamish's breath.

'Yes. She's the family black sheep. Hitch-hiked out of Doongabi when she was eighteen. Never married, never settled in one place. She's lived all over the world, seen all kinds of things and can swear in a dozen different languages. I have a postcard from every place she's ever been. I was five when I received my first one.'

Hamish nodded. 'And you knew you wanted to be just like her.'

'No.' Lola shook her head, her curls bounced. 'I knew I *was* just like her.' She gave a half-laugh. 'Poor Mum. I don't think she's ever forgiven May.'

'She sounds fabulous.'

'She is.' Lola's gaze fixed on the foam spraying over the bow and Hamish studied her profile, as gorgeous as the rest of her. 'I can see the bridge.' She pointed at the arch just coming into view and sighed. 'I never get tired of that sight.'

Hamish dragged his gaze off her face, following the line of her finger. But he didn't want to. He could look at Lola Fraser all damn day and never get tired of *that* sight either.

They alighted from the ferry at the North Sydney Wharf about fifteen minutes later. 'It's a few minutes' walk from here.'

Hamish fell in beside her as they sauntered down what looked very much like a suburban street. 'What suburb is this?'

'It's Kirribilli.'

'So the hospital's not far, then?'

'Um, yes. Up that way…somewhere.' She waved her hand vaguely in the general direction they were heading. 'At the dodgy end.'

Hamish laughed as they passed beautifully restored terraced houses, big gnarly trees that looked as if they'd been in the ground for a century and cars with expensive price tags. It was hard to believe this harbourside suburb—*any* harbourside suburb—had a dodgy end.

She turned right at an intersection. 'So, are you going to tell me what's so special about this street?'

'Nope.' Lola shook her head. 'You'll see soon enough.'

'Mystery woman, huh?'

She just shrugged and kept walking but there

was a bounce to her step. Like she couldn't wait to get there. Like *maybe* she couldn't wait to show him? It was intriguing that a woman who'd just confessed to having itchy feet and being a bit of a daredevil would choose a place so quiet and unassuming to take him.

They passed a park and Hamish could see down to the harbour again, glittering like a jewel and the massive motor boats moored at what looked like a marina. A personal trainer was putting a group of people through a session and a large gathering of people were picnicking under the shade of a tree.

'This,' she said as she turned left at another street, 'is my favourite place to visit in Sydney.'

Hamish turned the corner to discover an avenue of massive Jacaranda trees alive with colour. The dry, gnarly branches knotted and tangled together overhead to form a lilac canopy down the entire length of the street. A carpet of dropped, purple-blue flowers covered the road.

It was stunning. Toowoomba had plenty of Jacarandas as well but this avenue was something else, the trees all lined up together to create an accidental work of art. A sight so *purple* it was almost blinding.

The kind of purple usually only found on coral reefs or in magic forests.

He glanced at Lola. She'd taken her sunglasses off and was staring down the street with rapt attention, like she'd discovered it all over again. Like she was seeing it for the first time.

She switched her attention to him and caught Hamish staring at her, but she didn't seem to mind. 'Isn't it the most beautiful thing you've ever seen?'

It was. *She* was. Looking down the street like a kid staring at an avenue of Christmas trees just lit up for the season, giddy with the magic shimmering in the air.

And she'd shared it with him. This beautiful place she loved so much.

'Yes. It's stunning.' *Just like you.*

She smiled at him and for a crazy second he wanted to pull her close and kiss her. Kiss her in this place she'd taken nobody else, so every time she came here she'd remember that she'd taken *him*.

But he didn't. He just said, 'Shall we walk up and down a few times?'

She gave a half-laugh, a girly edge of excitement to it as he offered her his arm and she looped hers through it. 'I thought you'd never ask.'

They didn't speak for a while, just strolled along, admiring the scenery as lilac flowers floated down all around them, quiet as snow-fall. It was like walking in a purple wonder-land. He turned to tell her that as two almost luminescent blue-purple flowers drifting in the gentle harbour breeze landed in Lola's hair.

It couldn't have been more perfect. 'You have flowers in your hair.'

'So do you.' She stood on tippytoes and plucked out the trumpet-shaped blooms. Their eyes locked for a moment and Hamish's pulse spiked before she dragged her gaze to the flowers in her palm. 'Only in nature could you get this colour.'

She blew them both off her hand, her gaze tracking them as they fluttered to the ground. 'Where are mine?' she asked, fixing him with a gaze that was all business now.

Hamish lifted his hand to remove them then decided against it. 'Wait.' He pulled his phone out of his pocket. 'I think this needs a picture first.'

She rolled her eyes but acquiesced. 'I get to veto it if it's terrible.'

He took the pic, zooming in tight on her face but conscious of snapping the background blaze of purple too, of framing this woman just right. He took several in quick succession then handed over his phone for Lola to approve what he'd taken.

'They're all pretty good,' she said, her thumb swiping back and forth between them. 'Hard to screw up with that background, I guess.'

Hard to screw up with the *foreground* too.

'This one.' She handed the phone over. 'Can you send it to me?'

Hamish glanced at it. She'd chosen one he'd zoomed out on a little but she was smiling a big, crazy smile that went all the way to her eyes and squished her full cheeks into chipmunk cuteness. The flowers in her hair drew attention to its blonde bounciness and the way it brushed her shoulders drew attention to her fallen-down strap.

'Sure.' His fingers got busy as they walked on again.

'So, Grace's big brother...' She smiled at him. 'Have *you* travelled?'

'Sure. I'm afraid it's kinda tame compared to you.'

She rolled her eyes. 'It's not a competition.'

Hamish thought back to that first trip, a smile spreading across his face. 'I did a tour of the Greek Islands with some mates when I was nineteen. Got a snowglobe from every place we stopped.'

Lola blinked. 'A snowglobe?' *In Greece?*

'Yeah. You know, those terrible, tacky things they sell in tourist traps everywhere.'

Lola laughed. 'I know.'

'Had to get something to remember the best damn trip of my life.'

'The Greek islands are beautiful, aren't they? And the people are wonderful. So generous.'

His smile became a grin. 'You have no idea.'

'Oh, *really*?' She cocked an eyebrow at him. 'I take it you were a recipient of some generosity? Of the female kind maybe?'

He laughed. 'I lost my virginity in Mykonos.'

'Ah. Was she a local or one of the women on the tour?'

Hamish shook his head. 'She was Greek. The daughter of the innkeeper. She couldn't speak much English and all I could say was please, thank you, good morning and can I have some ouzo.'

She laughed. 'What else do you need?'

'Nothing, as it turned out.' Hamish laughed too. 'A little ouzo and good manners go a long way.'

'That's a great life motto,' she said as they crossed to the other side of the street, trampling a sea of fallen purple flowers. 'I don't suppose there was an *I lost my virginity in Mykonos* snowglobe?'

'No, sadly… I would have bought the hell out of that.'

Lola shook her head as they headed back the other way. 'Where else?'

'I did a tour of Europe the following year. Fifteen countries in twenty-five days.'

'Oh, God,' Lola groaned. 'This isn't where you tell me that you could only ever get laid on a tour so that's all you've ever done?'

'No.' He grinned. 'But it is surprising how… accommodating being on holiday makes a woman.'

'I would say that is most definitely true.'

Hamish didn't really want to think about how much travelling Lola had done and how much adrenaline she must have had to burn off after all her death-defying adventures. But he was jealous as hell of whoever had been in the right place at the right time to be the recipient of all that excess energy.

He knew how mind-blowing she was in grief. He could only begin to imagine how amazing she'd be pumped with devil-may-care.

'Since then I've been to LA and New York for brief visits. And to New Zealand for a ski trip last year.'

'Let me guess, you have snowglobes from all of them?'

'Absolutely. It's worth, like, fifty bucks, that collection.'

She laughed. 'And where's your favourite place out of everywhere you've been?'

'Well, Mykonos, obviously.'

He smiled and she rolled her eyes. '*Obviously.* What about your second favourite place?'

'London. I was only there for three days and I need to go back because I loved it. What about you? What's your number one pick of all the places you've been?'

She sucked in air through her teeth. 'That's a hard call.'

'I bet. But there must be something that just grabbed you by the gut?'

'Last year I went on a tandem hangglider flight over an Austrian lake. It was…magical. We hovered for so long, riding the air currents I actually felt like I was flying and the Alps in the distance were all snow-capped. It was almost…spiritual, you know?'

'It does sound spiritual but I'd rather get my thrills with both feet planted firmly on the ground.'

'Afraid of heights?'

Hamish's breath caught at the amusement in her voice. She was something else when she teased him. She wasn't flirting exactly but it felt good to have her green eyes dancing at him.

'Afraid of plunging to my death attached to some dude I don't know is more like it.'

She shrugged. 'Life's too short to worry about the what-ifs.'

'Maybe. But I tend to see all the disastrous things that go wrong for people indulging in high-risk ventures. I think it skews my view somewhat.'

'Hey, there are plenty of ICU patients who were doing risky things that didn't work out. But you could trip over your feet tomorrow, smack your head on the ground and die. Just getting out of bed each day is a risk.'

'Exactly.' Hamish grinned. 'Which is why I plan on dying in my bed at the grand old age of ninety-six after having sex with a beautiful woman.'

A smile played on her mouth as she stopped and looked up at him. 'Sex, huh? Wow, you do like to push the envelope.'

'Hey, sex at ninety-six *is* pushing the envelope.'

She laughed. 'Come on. Let's walk down again and keep going. There's a great little café that overlooks the harbour. We might not be able to get a seat but you don't know if you don't try, right?'

Hamish cocked an eyebrow. 'You even like to take risks with tables.'

'You really need to take a walk on the wild side, Hamish Gibson.'

Hamish grinned. He'd grown up around horses and cattle and farm machinery. He'd done his fair share of wild *and* stupid. He didn't feel like he had anything to prove. But Lola could probably persuade him to do anything. 'I'm starting to see the attraction.'

CHAPTER SIX

LOLA TRIED NOT to make too much noise the next morning as she crept down the hall of the silent apartment, tightening the knot on her short gown. Hamish was on a couple of days of orientation so he didn't start till nine but she didn't want to disturb him at five thirty in the morning with her fridge opening and toast popping and teaspoon clinking.

Grace had always been a light sleeper and Lola figured it probably ran in the Gibson family. Her parents were the same so she knew it was a *country* thing. She needn't have worried, though. Her toast had just popped when she heard the front door open and a sweaty Hamish appeared a few moments later, his damp shorts and shirt clinging to him.

'Is that coffee?'

Lola nodded, lost for words both at his appearance and the fact he was not only out of bed but had already been for a *run*.

Who was he?

'Is there enough for two?'

Lola nodded again, still finding it difficult to locate adequate speech. His pheromones wafted to her on a wave of healthy sweat and she leaned against the kitchen bench as her legs weakened in an exceedingly unhelpful way. She ground her feet into the floor to stop herself launching at him.

'Can you pour me one? I'll just have a quick shower.'

And then she was looking at empty space, the tang of salt in the air a tangible reminder he *had* been here, an image in her head of Hamish in the shower a reminder of where he *was* right now.

Lola hoped like hell these shower fantasies weren't going to be a regular thing.

Determined to think of something else, her mind drifted to Hamish's confession about his virginity. The fact he still enjoyed the memory in a sexily smug way over ten years later was either testament to the greatness of the event or the depth of his gratitude. Both were endearing as all giddy-up.

Was it crazy to feel a tiny bit jealous of the woman on Mykonos?

She'd lost her virginity travelling too. She'd been eighteen and in Phuket where she'd met a backpacker called Jeremy. He'd been exotically handsome—Eurasian with a sexy Brit accent—and had known it. But she hadn't cared. She'd wanted to show her parents and everyone in Doongabi she was sophisticated and worldly. Plus there'd been cheap beer and a little too much sun earlier in the day.

Lola didn't remember a lot of it. Unlike Hamish, who appeared to remember his first time in great detail. She wondered if Jeremy still thought about that night with the same mix of pleasure and reminiscence that Hamish obviously did. How awesome would it be, knowing there was a guy out there in the world who got a secret, goofy grin every time he thought about his first time with you?

Knowing that you'd rocked his world?

She thought about that note again, the one Hamish had left for her the morning after, with its goofy smiley face. Did he smile like that whenever he thought about what *they'd* done together?

Had she been as *unforgettable* as he'd claimed?

Hamish reappeared fifteen minutes later as she sat in front of the TV, listening to the morning news, And, hell, he looked seriously hot in his uniform. Like a freaking action man in his multi-pocketed lightweight overalls with a utility belt crammed with all the bits and bobs a paramedic needed on the road.

He looked strong and capable. Wide shoulders, wavy cinnamon hair with a sprinkle of ginger, powerful thighs. He looked like he could fix anything—*anyone*—and Lola's heart fluttered just looking at him. When he plonked himself down next to her on the couch—the same couch where they'd done *it*—any hope of following the news reports was dashed.

Lola took a sip of her coffee. 'Are you nervous? About your first day?'

He seemed to consider the question for a beat or two. 'Not of the work. I know Toowoomba may seem like a country backwater compared to the size and population of Sydney, but it's a decent-sized regional city and I've seen a lot on the job. I *am* nervous about the people I'm going to be working with. I don't know anyone so I'm not sure who knows what and who to be wary of.'

Lola nodded. Finding out colleagues' levels of experience and their limitations always took a little time. Sometimes that could be detrimental, especially in emergency situations.

'Well, if it helps, I know quite a few of the paramedics stationed at Kirribilli. They all seem professional and they all get along, work as a team. A lot of them go to Billi's after their shift. Make sure you go along. It's a great place to de-stress.'

It was also a great place to pick up women—as he would know. The sudden thought was like a hot knife sliding between her ribs as she thought about him hooking up at Billi's, bringing her back here. Which was crazy. He could sleep with every woman in Sydney if he wanted to—it wasn't any of her business or her concern.

'Right. Well...' She stood. 'I'd better get ready.'

She didn't wait for his reply, scooping her plate off the coffee table and heading to the kitchen. She was going to be late if she didn't hustle.

Lola had another busy morning with Emma. The condition of her heart was worsening. Her body was becoming more oedematous which was putting pressure on other organs. Even the conjunctivas of her eyes bulged with oedema, requiring frequent ointment to prevent them drying.

The specialists were now at the stage where they were talking about a transplant. The question, though, was whether they could stabilise Emma enough to survive the rigors of such a massive operation and if they could, how long could they keep her heart going in its current state while they waited for another to become available?

Sadly, they didn't grow on trees. Even an emergency listing could still sometimes take weeks. And nobody was confident Emma's heart could last that long.

Her family were beside themselves with worry and Lola spent a lot of the morning trying to meet their growing need for comfort, assurance and answers. Lola could give the first and she did, she just wished she could give the other two as well.

At least Barry was more comfortable about being near Emma now. He'd grown more confident and had taken to reading out all the supportive messages that family and friends had left for Emma on social media. There were hundreds every day and Lola knew the outpouring was not only good for Emma to hear but for Barry and her parents as well.

'I think she *can* hear me,' Barry said.

Lola smiled and nodded. 'I do too.' She'd noticed how Emma's heart rate settled a little every time Barry or her parents touched and talked to her. 'Keep it up.'

By the time Lola was heading to lunch she felt like she'd been working for a week. Seeing Grace in the kitchen alcove of the deserted staffroom was a fabulous rejuvenator.

'Hey, you here with the team?' Lola asked as she threw a tea bag into her mug and filled it with hot water from the boiler attached to the wall. Although she was the renal transplant co-ordinator, Grace often stepped in when a co-ordinator from a different department was on annual leave.

Grace nodded, following Lola's lead and also filling her mug. 'Just finished the Emma Green meeting. You're looking after her?'

Lola settled her butt against the edge of the kitchen counter. 'Yep.'

Grace settled hers beside Lola's. 'She's not doing very well, is she?'

Lola shook her head as she blew on her hot tea. 'No. She's going backwards at the moment, which is a worry.' Emma's chances of survival decreased every minute they couldn't stabilise her condition. 'She's just about reached maximum drug support.'

'Do you think she'll stabilise?'

It wasn't an unusual question to ask. Experienced nurses often had gut feelings about patients. 'Well, her body's been pummelled over the years so… But she's got this far. She's obviously a fighter. I just…don't know.' Lola took a sip of her tea. 'Are they going to list her?'

Lola knew they didn't list people just on the gut feeling of the nurses. But she also knew that if Emma pulled through, if she stabilised, she was going to need a transplant because she couldn't stay on life support for ever and she couldn't survive without it. Unless she had a new heart.

Grace sipped her tea. 'The team is discussing it now.'

'Good.' Relief flowed through Lola's core and she smiled. 'Fingers crossed.'

They sipped at their tea for a moment or two. 'Hamish tells me you took him to see the jacarandas yesterday.'

Lola was instantly on guard, not fooled by Grace's casual slouch against the bench. 'Yes.'

One elegantly arched eyebrow lifted. 'I thought that was a state secret?'

'I told you about it,' Lola protested, dropping her gaze to the surface of her tea.

Grace regarded her over the rim of her cup, speculation coming off her in waves, even though Lola was finding the depths of her tea utterly fascinating.

'He's going back to Toowoomba, Lola.'

'I know.'

'And then he's moving to a rural post.'

'I know.'

'And you're not interested in settling down, remember?'

'I know.'

She wasn't. There were still places to go and people she hadn't met yet. And she couldn't do that being with Hamish in some rural outpost somewhere.

'Lola?'

Lola almost cringed at *that* note in her friend's voice—that mix of suspicion and dawning knowledge were a deadly accurate cocktail. She girded her loins to look directly at Grace as if she and Hamish hadn't got naked and done the wild thing already and this conversation wasn't too late.

'I said I know, Grace. Take a chill pill.' Lola plastered a smile on her face. 'He wanted to know my favourite spot in Sydney and I figured a country boy would probably appreciate some nature.'

Grace studied her closely. 'But *you* went with him.'

Lola shifted uncomfortably under her friend's all-seeing gaze. 'I haven't seen it yet this year. Plus, he's your brother. I thought it might be…polite to play tour guide.'

The expression on Grace's face finally cleared and she nodded slowly, as if she'd reached her conclusion. She glanced around to make sure no one had slipped into the room unnoticed while they'd been deep in conversation. 'You two have *slept* together.'

It wasn't a question and it took all Lola's willpower not to glance away, to hold her friend's gaze and brazen it out. 'Don't be ridiculous. He's been here two nights during which we have *not* slept together.'

Which was the truth.

'No.' Grace slowly shook her head. 'Not this time. Last time.'

Oh, hell. Grace had missed her calling as a PI. 'As if I would sleep with Hamish.' Lola lowered her voice. 'He's your *brother.*'

Grace waved a hand. 'I don't care about that.'

Lola blinked at Grace's easy dismissal. She'd thought her friend would care but it ultimately didn't matter—*Lola* cared.

That was what mattered.

'I care about the fact that while you two are exactly alike in a lot of ways, you want completely different things, which means that you're both going to get hurt and that I'm going to be in the middle of it all.'

Lola had to admire how well Grace could summarise things. 'There's nothing going on, Grace.'

Another *almost* truth. There *was* an undercurrent between them but they weren't acting on it. And that was the most important thing.

'Lola?'

For a brief second, the sudden appearance of one of the shift runners was a welcome relief until concern spiked Lola's pulse. 'Emma?'

'No, sorry, she's okay. Just thought you'd like to know Dr Wright is heading in to talk to the family now.'

'Is he?' She plonked the mostly untouched mug on the bench. 'Sorry,' she said to Grace. 'I've gotta go.'

'Isn't this your lunch break?'

Lola nodded. 'But I have to sit in on it.'

She hated it when the doctors had a family conference without the nurse present. Invariably a patient's loved ones only heard some of the conversation or misheard it or didn't understand it but nodded along anyway because they were too overwhelmed by everything. When they had questions later—and they always had questions later—Lola could answer them, could reiterate what the doctor had said exactly, could interpret *and* correct any misperceptions.

But only *if* she was privy to what had been discussed.

Grace nodded. 'That's fine. Go. I'll pop around later this afternoon after I have some

ducks in a row and introduce myself to the
family.'

'Okay. Thanks.' Lola scuttled off to the conference room.

Lola was on her second glass of wine on the
balcony when she heard the front door open.
Her pulse spiked followed by a quick stab of
annoyance. She had to stop this stupid behav-
iour around him, for crying out loud.

Why couldn't she just look at him and think,
Oh, a guy I once slept with, and act normal.
Instead of, *Holy cow, a guy I once slept with.
Danger! Danger! Danger!* Why was having to
deal with him again after they'd got naked and
done the wild thing *such* a problem?

She usually handled the ex-lover stuff really well.

It was probably just the newness of the situation. It'd only been a few days since Hamish
had come to stay after all. She probably just
needed time to get used to their living arrangements.

Of course, Grace's speculation about them
hadn't helped. Lola hadn't had much of a
chance to think about the implications of that
during the remainder of her shift but she'd been
thinking about it plenty since. She should have
known Grace would guess something was

going on. They may not have been besties since kindergarten, but they had known each other for several years and had lived together for the last two.

Of course Grace could read her like a book.

Which meant she was going to have to give Hamish a heads-up, because Lola had no doubt Grace would soon be seeking an explanation from her brother.

And she needed to get ahead of that.

Despite the inner uproar at the thought and Hamish's tread getting closer and closer, Lola forced herself to stay right where she was, her feet casually up on the railing of the balcony. They at least weren't throbbing any more after her long, busy day with Emma. A good soak in a bath had helped.

So had the wine.

'Hey.'

'Hey.' Lola plastered a smile on her face as she half turned in her seat.

He stepped onto the balcony, returning her smile, his gaze shifting to her legs before quickly shifting back again.

'How was orientation?'

He gave a half-laugh as he undid his utility belt and discarded it on the table with a dull thud. 'Let's just say I can't wait to get out on the road.'

Lola nodded. Orientation days were generally tedious. They were a necessary evil and HR boffins loved them, but staring at a bunch of policy and procedure manuals all day was not fun for most people.

He pulled up the chair beside her, turned it around and plonked himself in it, raising his feet to the railing also, his legs outstretched. Fabric pulled taut across powerful thighs as he crossed his feet at the ankles. Lola fixed her gaze on the darkening outline of the Norfolk pine in the park opposite.

'Met my partner, though. A woman called Jenny Bell. She seems good. Know her?'

Lola nodded. 'Yeah. She's an excellent intensive care paramedic. One of the best.'

'Good.' He dropped his head from side to side to stretch out his traps. 'How was your shift?'

'Long.' She took a sip of her wine, resolutely pushing worry for Emma out of her mind. 'One of those shifts where you're on your toes every second.'

'Well, I've been sitting on my ass all day, so I can cook us something to eat if you like.'

Lola blinked at the unexpected offer. 'You can cook?'

'Well...' He smiled. 'Nothing too gourmet but I manage.'

'Good to know. But—' Lola grabbed a menu off the table she'd been studying earlier. 'Let's just order something gourmet and get it delivered for tonight.'

He took the menu and opened it. 'Delivered, huh?'

Lola laughed. 'Yeah, *Country*, it's a city thing. Choose something from the extensive menu then I order it through an app and a nice person delivers it right to the door.'

'I like the sound of that.'

They chose some pasta and garlic bread and Lola ordered it online. 'Should be here in thirty.'

'Good.' He stood and reached for his utility belt. 'I'll take a shower.'

Lola shut her eyes against a sudden welling of images in her head. *Enough with the shower already.*

At least she knew something that could combat the seduction of those images this time. 'Before you go…'

He paused, belt in hand, his gaze meeting hers. 'What?'

Lola sighed. Damn Grace's observation skills for putting her in this position. 'Look, I know I said we weren't to speak of this again but…'

'But?' Two cinnamon eyebrows rose in query.

She let out a breath. *Just say it!* 'Your sister knows we slept together.'

His face went blank for a second before his eyebrows lifted in surprise this time. 'You told Grace we slept together?'

'No.' Lola shook her head. 'Not exactly. She kinda guessed.'

'Ah. Yeah…she's like a bulldog when she scents blood.'

'I denied it. Told her there wasn't anything going on but… I'm sure you'll be hearing from her so I thought you might like some prior notice.'

'I have a missed call from her actually. I was going to ring her soon.'

'Well…that's probably why.'

He gave a soft snort. 'She always was one of those pain-in-the-ass, know-it-all little sisters.'

Lola laughed. 'Well, like I said, I did deny it. I just don't think she believed me so…sorry if you cop some flak from her.'

'Don't worry.' He grinned. 'I know how to handle Gracie.'

In Lola's experience men tended to underestimate a woman's tenacity when her mind was made up but that was between him and his sister and, to be honest, it was good to be able to pass that hot potato on to someone else.

'All right. I'll hit the shower.'

She didn't watch him go. She stared straight ahead at the trees silhouetted against a velvety purple sky. Did he *have* to constantly announce his intention to take a shower? Couldn't he just go and do it without informing her all the time?

Planting images in her head. Naked images. Wet images.

It was going to be a very long two months.

CHAPTER SEVEN

A FEW WEEKS later Hamish was sitting in the work vehicle, eating lunch under a shady tree. It was exceptionally hot today and they were between jobs. He was flicking through images on his phone to show Jenny some pictures of the feed lot his family ran back in Toowoomba. He came across the one he'd taken of Lola that day with jacaranda flowers in her hair and smiled.

Things had been a little weird to start with between them but they seemed to have settled down into an easy kind of co-existence. It wasn't the flirty banter of their relationship a few months ago, or sex on the couch, which he probably wouldn't say no to, but it was something he could walk away from when his time in Sydney was up.

Because the more he got to know Lola, the more he knew, she was city right down to her bootstraps. And it didn't matter how *wicked* his thoughts got alone in his room each night, Lola wasn't going country for anyone.

Just then a call came over the radio and Jenny threw the last of her sandwich down her neck. 'Buckle up,' she said as they climbed into the vehicle and she flicked on the siren.

Hamish turned his phone off, shutting down thoughts of Lola as adrenaline flushed into his system and he concentrated on that as they screamed through the Sydney streets.

They arrived at the home of a fifty-six-year-old man called Robert twelve minutes later. He'd had a probable MI—myocardial infarction or heart attack. He had no pulse and wasn't breathing.

It was Hamish and Jenny's second of the day. The heat wave they were experiencing was no doubt contributing to that.

Two advanced care paramedics were already on scene. They'd arrived six minutes previously and were administering CPR, having taken over from the patient's wife and a neighbour who was a nurse.

The fact that Robert had had lifesaving measures carried out immediately on collapsing could probably mean the difference between him dying today and living.

Jenny quickly intubated the patient and stayed at the head, delivering puffs of oxygen into Robert's lungs via the breathing tube, while one of the advanced care paramedics, another woman, continued to do compressions. The other was busy inserting a couple of intravenous lines and Hamish was managing the emergency drugs and the defibrillator, which had already been connected when they'd arrived.

'Recommends another shock,' he said, as he flipped the lids on another mini-jet of adrenaline and wiped his brow with his forearm. It was stiflingly hot in the little, inner-suburban shoebox house.

Jenny gave a few quick hyper-inflating puffs of oxygen before she joined the others, who had shuffled out of contact with the body. 'All clear,' Hamish called, double checking everyone was away before he pushed the button and delivered the recommended shock.

The patient's body jerked slightly—not quite like the dramatic arch seen on TV shows—and all eyes watched the heart trace on the monitor.

A hot flood of relief washed over Hamish as the previous frenetic, squiggly line suddenly flipped into an organised pattern. 'Sinus tachy,' he announced, although he didn't need to. Everyone there knew how to read an ECG trace.

Jenny and the other female paramedic high-fived before she said, 'Okay, let's get him locked and loaded.'

They'd revived the patient, brought Robert back from the brink, but heart-attack patients were notoriously unstable in the hours immediately after the heart muscle dying, which meant Robert needed a tertiary care facility pronto. Somewhere with a cath lab, a cardiac surgeon and an intensive care unit.

'We'll take him to Kirribilli General,' Jenny said.

They unloaded the patient in the emergency department twenty minutes later. Hamish listened to Jenny's rapid-fire handover to the team. Lola was right, she was an excellent paramedic.

'I wonder where the third one's going to be,' Hamish said as they headed back to the ambulance.

Because these things tended to come in threes.

'Somewhere with air-con, I hope,' Jenny quipped.

Hamish laughed. It was nice working with someone who was not only good at their job but also knew how to make light of a situation.

It was the kind of job that needed it.

A call came over the radio as soon as they

were seated. Another suspected MI. 'No rest for the wicked,' Jenny said, flicking the sirens on.

And Hamish's thoughts went straight to Lola.

Hamish sighed as he entered the apartment later that evening. It was good to be home. It was still warm outside but their apartment was getting a nice breeze from the direction of the beach and Lola had all the doors and windows open to catch it.

The sheer curtain at the sliding door to the balcony was billowing with it and Lola was shimmying in the kitchen to some music she was obviously listening to via her ear buds. She had her back to him as she stood at the counter, a bottle of beer in one hand and a fork in the other, attacking a container of leftover Chinese takeaway.

She'd obviously had a shower. Her hair was wet and she was wearing her short gown that brushed her legs at mid-thigh. He didn't know for sure what she wore underneath it but he had spent a lot of time speculating over it.

Tank top and lacy thong were his current picks.

She looked cool and relaxed and was a sight for sore eyes after a long day. Something he wouldn't mind coming home to every day, in fact…

He shoved his shoulder against the door-frame. 'You're chipper today.'

She startled and whipped around. 'Bloody hell, Hamish. You scared the living daylights out of me.'

She brought the hand holding her beer to her chest and Hamish's temperature kicked up a notch as the action pulled the gown taut across her cleavage and the tight buds of two erect nipples.

He dragged his gaze upwards. 'Is your patient improving?'

Lola had told him about the woman waiting for a heart transplant. Not any particulars of her identity, just her situation, and he could tell by how fondly she talked about the family and how often she seemed to be assigned to the case that this particular patient had slipped under Lola's barriers.

A hazard of the job. He'd been there himself.

'Yeah.' She grinned as she pulled her ear buds out and her face lit up. His breath hitched. 'She's really turned a corner. She's coming along in leaps and bounds now. Still needs a heart, of course, but...'

Hamish nodded. The imminent threat to her life had passed but she needed a transplant to survive going forward. He hoped she got one and that the family got something extra-special to celebrate as the festive season approached. Even if it meant some other family would have the worst Christmas of their life.

He remembered when his sister-in-law, Merridy, had got her kidney. In her case, his brother Lachlan had fortunately been a tissue match for her and had been able to donate one of his. What a joy, a relief, it had been, knowing they hadn't had to wait for somebody to die to give Merridy that gift. But also how sobering it had been for everyone, knowing that others weren't so lucky.

'You're drinking beer?' He'd only ever seen her drinking wine.

Why was there something hot about a chick drinking beer?

'That's because it's *Die Hard* marathon night.'

Hamish laughed. 'And that requires beer?'

She rolled her eyes. 'You think John MacClane drinks Sauvignon Blanc?'

'I wouldn't think so.' They both smiled and Hamish ground his feet into the floor as the urge to walk over and kiss her almost overwhelmed him. 'I thought we were out of beer? I meant to get some on my way home.'

'I picked some up from the liquor warehouse on my way home.'

Hamish grimaced. That place gave him the

willies. A football stadium of booze was mind-boggling. 'Rather you than me.'

'It's okay, *Country*.' A smile hovered on her mouth. 'I know you don't get shops that big where you come from. I've got your back.'

Hamish laughed. Her teasing set a warm glow in the centre of his chest. 'Toowoomba isn't exactly a two-horse town. It's a fairly decent size.'

'You're going to be moving to a two-horse town, though, right? Once your course is done?'

'Hopefully. Those jobs don't come up very often. People don't tend to leave them once they're in.' Hamish laughed at her visible shudder. 'Newsflash, *City*, some people like living in small towns.'

'If you say so.'

'Plus, it's a professional challenge. Out there, it'll be just me on shift, no back-up. The next ambulance service could be a couple of hundred kilometres away.'

'Sounds terrifying.'

'Nah. There'll be a doctor and Flying Doctor back-up but the autonomy...the skills I'll acquire can only make me a better paramedic.'

'I think that would drive me nuts. I like working with a team. I thrive on being a small part in a well-oiled machine. I like the people

I work with. I enjoy their company. I wouldn't want to work in isolation.'

Hamish shrugged. 'I don't want to do it for ever necessarily. But I'd like to do it for a while.' Clearly, though, she didn't. And it bothered him more than it should have.

'Well...' She looked at him like he was a little crazy. 'Each to their own, I guess.' She took a slug of her beer. 'Are you joining me tonight?'

'*Die Hard* marathon?' He grinned, shaking off the urban-rural divide between them. 'Absolutely! I'll just have a shower.'

She nodded. 'I'll pop the corn.'

Lola watched him go. Good Lord! The man took more showers than a teenage boy who'd just discovered the Victoria's Secret catalogue. Which led her down a whole other path she did not want to go...

She got busy in the kitchen instead, putting the popcorn bag in the microwave and grabbing two frosty long-necked bottles out of the fridge. When her mind started to wander to his shower, she distracted herself by rereading the latest postcard from May stuck on the fridge. She was in Mongolia, the usual *Wish you were here* in her lovely loopy handwriting making Lola smile.

By the time the popcorn had popped and

been decanted into a bowl, Lola had cracked the lids off the beers, and the first movie was queued, Hamish was out of the shower. He reappeared in a T-shirt and loose basketball shorts that fell to just above his knee but clung a little due to the humidity.

It was what he usually wore after his shower— just a little more indecent tonight.

But that wasn't a particularly helpful thought right now as he stood there, temptation incarnate, his hair damp and curling against his neck. She had to remind herself that this *thing* she felt could go nowhere.

That they lived very different lives. Wanted very different things.

Still, the lights were out and the glow from the television caught the ginger highlights of his stubbly jawline and he smelled like coconut and the deodorant he used that reminded her of fresh Alpine air, heavy with the scent of pine.

How could a man smell like the beach and the Alps all at once?

'Beer?' Lola thrust a long-necked bottle at him.

'You read my mind.'

He took it from her and they clinked. He took a pull of his as he sat beside her, the popcorn bowl between them. It was a large bowl but it still put him closer than was good for her sanity. Of course, if he thought about what they'd done on this couch half as much as she did, no amount of space was adequate.

'Okay, roll it,' he said.

Lola laughed and pressed 'play', taking a long cool swallow of her beer as the credits did their thing. She could do this. She could sit here on this couch with Hamish, where they'd done the wild thing a few months ago, and watch one of her favourite movies as if they'd never laid hands on each other.

A sudden thought occurred to her and she turned to face him slightly. 'You *are* a *Die Hard* fan, right?'

He smiled and her heart skipped a beat as he raised his bottle to her. 'Yippie-ki-yay.' He tapped it against hers again and settled back against the couch, grabbing a handful of popcorn.

Lola was so damn happy she actually sighed.

After two of the most entertaining hours of her life, Lola was sad to see the end of the movie. Normally she and Grace just sat and watched it, gobbling it up like they gobbled the popcorn. But Hamish was a much more active consumer. He kept up a running commentary of interesting asides about the films or the actors and mimicked his favourite lines, even adlib-bing better ones.

They'd also had a serious discussion about it being a rom-com. He'd been horrified in an en-dearingly masculine way when Lola had dared to suggest it.

'Well…thank you very much for your insights into the movie,' he said, as Lola hit 'stop' on the DVD remote. 'They're wrong, of course…' his lips quirked '…but it's given me a whole different perspective on it.'

Lola laughed and threw a kernel of popcorn at him. It was a spontaneous thing that fitted the mood of the moment but one she regretted immediately as the glitter of laughter in his eyes changed to a competitive gleam.

'Oh, it's going to be like that, is it?' He dug into their second bowl of popcorn and grabbed a handful of kernels.

'Hamish.'

If he heard the warning note in her voice he chose to ignore it as he slowly lifted his hand above her head.

'Don't you *dare*.'

He just smiled and opened it. Popcorn fell around her like snow. When they settled he plucked one out of her hair and ate it, his eyes goading her to do something about it.

'Right.' She grinned at him, plunging both

hands into the frothing bowl and coming out with two fistfuls. 'You asked for it.'

He laughed, which only encouraged her further. He was prepared to swerve and duck, obviously, but not prepared for her to grab his T-shirt and dump the popcorn down his front.

'Well, now,' Hamish muttered, 'this is war.'

He reached for the front of her gown with one hand and the popcorn with the other. Lola half laughed, half squealed, flinging herself back, trying to twist away, but Hamish was bigger and stronger and more determined, laughing as he followed her down, sending the popcorn bowl flying as he anchored her squirming body to the couch and stuffed a handful of kernels down the front of her gown.

Lola joined him in laughter as the popcorn scratched against her skin. She tried to remove it but he just shook his head and said, 'Nuh-uh,' as he grabbed her hands.

They were both panting and laughing hard from their playful struggle so it took a moment to register that he had her well and truly pinned, his hips over hers, one big thigh shoved between her legs, his hands entwined in hers above their heads.

He seemed to realise at the same time, the glitter in his eyes different now—not light or teasing.

Darker. Hotter.

Their gazes locked and Lola's heart punched against her rib cage, nothing but the sounds of their breathing between them now. Panting had turned into something rougher, more needy as she stared at him looming over her. An ache roared to life between her legs, right where his knee was shoved, and she couldn't fight the urge to squirm against the pressure to relieve the ache.

His eyes widened at the action and he pressed his knee against her harder. She gasped at the heat and friction building between her legs and he pushed again.

'Lola,' he muttered, his breathing as rough as sandpaper, his gaze boring into hers. Then, as if something had snapped, he swooped down and kissed her.

Lola flared like a lit match beneath the onslaught, moaning his name. Her hands, suddenly free from his, slid into the back of his hair, holding him there. His hands found her hips, gripping them tight as he ground his knee against her over and over.

Lights popped and flared behind Lola's eyes, her whole world melting down as his mouth and his body worked hers. She was hot, too hot, and her heart was beating too fast. There were too many clothes. She wanted them gone. Wanted them off. Wanted him naked and inside her, pounding away, calling her name.

She reached down between them for his shorts, needing them gone while she could still think, while his kisses hadn't quite stolen her capacity to participate. Her hand connected with his erection and she made a triumphant noise at the back of her throat as she grabbed it and fondled him through his shorts. He groaned, breaking off the kiss, dropping his forehead to her neck, his lips warm against the frantic beat of her pulse at the base of her throat.

He was big and hard and solid in her hand. She squeezed him and he swore into her neck, his voice like gravel, his breath a hot caress.

This. She wanted this. Him. Inside her. Right where his knee was pressed tight and hard.

Lola moved her hand to his waistband, sliding her fingers beneath it, her pulse so loud in her ears it was like Niagara Falls inside her head. But before she hit her objective, his big hand clamped around her wrist.

'Wait.'

He panted into her neck for a few more moments, his body a dead weight on top of hers. Lola also panted, blinking into the dark room, grappling with the sudden cessation of endorphins, confused yet still craving at the same time.

He eased himself up a little, his hand still shackling her wrist. 'Are you sure about this, Lola?'

His gaze bored into hers once again and she could see he was struggling with this as much as she was. His arousal was as obvious in his eyes as it had been in her hand. But there was conflict there as well.

'Because if we keep going like this we'll end up having sex on this couch again, and I'm telling you now I don't think I can go back to being just roomies again if we do.'

The implication of his words slowly sank in, the sexual buzz fizzling as Lola's brain started to kick in. It was like a cold bucket of water.

But it was the cold bucket of water she needed.

'Right.' She nodded and pulled her hand out of his, her breathing erratic. What the hell had she been thinking? 'Of course. Sorry... I...' She trailed off because she didn't have any kind of adequate explanation for what the hell had just happened.

'Don't worry about it. It's fine.' He rolled off her, his butt sliding to the floor, his back against the couch.

'No…it's not,' she said breathily, her hands shaking a little. He was right, they'd overstepped their boundary. And they probably needed to re-establish it. 'I think we need to talk about it.'

'Okay.'

He didn't turn and perversely Lola wanted him to turn and look at her. And, *Lordy*, she wanted to touch him.

She didn't.

'It wouldn't work out between you and me. No matter how good the sex is. We have different jobs and different lives and different *goals*.'

He nodded. 'I know.'

'I'm sorry that we got carried away but I think we both need to agree that if this living arrangement is to work out, we just can't go there.'

He nodded again before rising to his feet. He was looking down at her but his eyes were too hooded in the semi-darkness to really see what he was feeling. He shoved a hand through his hair. 'You're right.'

Lola reached for his hand but he pulled back slightly and it felt like a slap to the face. 'I'm sorry,' she whispered once more.

'Me too,' he whispered back then stepped away, feet crunching over popcorn as he headed to his room.

CHAPTER EIGHT

NOVEMBER MORPHED INTO DECEMBER. The weather got hotter, the days longer. The Christmas tree had gone up in the apartment. Hamish had been in Sydney for five weeks and was working his first run of night shifts. He didn't mind working nights usually, he was a good sleeper and night shift in Sydney was a hell of a lot busier than back home. Which was great—there was nothing more tiring than trying to fill in twelve empty hours.

But Lola was also working nights, which meant they were home together during the day. *Sleeping.* A much bigger psychological temptation than being at home together and sleeping during the night.

Because the night was for sleeping. And being in bed during the day felt decadent. Like flying first class or a good bottle of cognac. Or daytime sex.

Totally and utterly *decadent*.

They weren't having daytime sex, of course. They weren't having *any* sex, thanks to their conversation after things had got out of hand on movie night. She was right, their lives were going in different directions and he respected that.

But it didn't help him sleep any better.

Having Lola just across the hallway from him was far too distracting. Sure as hell *not* conducive to sleep. Not conducive to night shifts. Not conducive to being a safe practitioner when he was so damn tired when he was on shift he couldn't think straight.

Consequently, Hamish wasn't looking forward to heading home in a few hours to repeat the whole not-sleeping process again. But it was his third night. Maybe if he was tired enough he could sleep despite the temptation of Lola in the next room.

Hamish's thoughts were interrupted by a squawk from his radio. 'Damn,' Jenny grumbled. It was almost two in the morning, they'd been going since they'd clocked on at eight and they'd only just left the hospital from their last emergency room drop-off. 'Are we ever going to get a chance for a cup of coffee tonight?'

But her grumbles quickly ceased when the seriousness of the call became evident. Some kind of explosion had happened in a night club in Kings Cross. It was a Saturday night in one of the city's oldest club districts. 'We have a mass casualty incident. Repeat mass casualty. Multiple fatalities, multiple victims. Code one please.'

Code one. Lights and sirens.

Neither Hamish nor Jenny needed to be told that. As intensive care paramedics, all their jobs were lights and sirens, but the urgency in the voice on the other end of the radio painted a pretty grim picture.

Jenny flicked on the siren. 'Hold onto your hat.'

Hamish had never seen anything like what greeted them when they arrived on scene twelve minutes later. A cacophony of sirens from a cavalcade of arriving emergency services vehicles—police, fire and ambulance, including several intensive care cars—*whooped* into the warm night air. The area had been cordoned off and over two dozen firemen were battling the blaze that currently forked out of the windows on the upper storey.

Others were running in and out of the lower floor, evacuating victims, masks in place to protect them from the smoke that billowed from the blown-out windows. It hung in the air, clogging Hamish's nose and stinging his eyes.

He and Jenny, their fully loaded packs in hand, reported to the scene controller. 'Some kind of incendiary device, although we won't know for sure until afterwards. Blast killed several people instantly and started a fire on the first floor, panic caused a stampede and the upper balcony collapsed under the weight of people trying to get out. The night club was packed to the gills, so we're talking at least a couple of hundred people.'

Hamish glanced around the scene as evacuated victims huddled in groups across the road from the night club. Some stood and some sat as they stared dazedly at the building, their faces bloodied, their clothes ripped. A lot of them were crying, some quietly in a kind of despair, others loudly in shock and rage and disbelief, railing against the police who had been tasked to question them and stop them from running back into the building to find their mates.

An incendiary device?

Someone had done this deliberately?

'Go to the triage station. There are several red tags there and more coming out all the time. The collapse has trapped quite a few people and the rescue squad are digging them out.'

'Red tag' referred to the colour system employed in mass casualty events to prioritise treatment. Everyone in the triage section would be tagged with a colour. Green for the walking wounded, yellow for stable but requiring observation, white for minor injury not requiring medical assistance.

And black. For the deceased.

Red identified patients who couldn't survive without immediate attention but still had survivable injuries.

Hamish followed Jenny down the street, adrenaline pumping through his system at the job ahead. He slowed as he passed an area that was obviously being used as a temporary morgue, a tarp being erected to shield the scene from the television cameras already vying for the most grisly footage. He didn't need to see them to know the dozen or so bodies lying under the sheets would be wearing black tags.

He glanced away, concentrating on what was ahead of them, not behind. On the people he could help, not the ones he couldn't. If he went there now, if he started thinking about such a senseless waste of life, about the horror of it, he'd get too angry to be of any use. He needed to channel his adrenaline, harness it for the hours ahead, not burn it all up in his rage.

A dozen paramedics, their reflective stripes glowing in the flare of emergency sirens, were working their way through the victims when they pulled up at triage. Jenny introduced both of them to the senior paramedic in charge. She calmly and efficiently pointed them to a section where two other intensive care paramedics were currently working among half a dozen casualties. 'Over there, please.'

Jenny shook her head in dismay as they made their way over. 'Who would do this?'

Hamish didn't have an answer, he was still grappling with it himself.

They got to work, steadily treating the red cards—establishing airways, treating haemorrhages and burns, getting access for fluids and drugs. In two hours Hamish had intubated four patients who hadn't looked much older than twenty and dispatched them for transport to one of the many hospitals around the city that had already activated their mass casualty protocols.

He'd hadn't been able to save two people and they'd died despite his attempts to treat their life-threatening injuries.

One, a girl wearing an 'Eighteen today' sash across her purple dress, was going to haunt his dreams, he just knew it. The dress was the colour of Lola's jacarandas, with the exception of the bright crimson blood spray across the front.

'Help me.' That's what she'd said to him, her eyes large and frightened, just before blood had welled up her throat and she'd coughed and spluttered and the light had drained from her eyes as she'd lost consciousness.

Hamish had worked frantically on her to staunch the bleeding, to stabilise her enough to get her to hospital, but he hadn't been able to save her.

He hadn't even known her name.

In all probability the chunk of whatever the hell had hit her chest had probably ruptured something major. What she'd needed had been a cardiothoracic surgeon and an operating theatre. What she'd got had been him.

And he hadn't been enough.

'This is the last of them,' a female voice said.

Hamish looked up from the chest tube he was taping into place, surprised to realise that dawn had broken. He hadn't noticed. Just as he hadn't noticed the stench of smoke in the air any more or the constant background wail of sirens as they came and went from the scene.

He'd shut everything out as he'd lurched from one person to the next, concentrating only on the one in front of him.

Two rescue squad officers, a male and the female who'd spoken, placed a stretcher bearing a long, lanky male on the ground. He was sporting an oxygen mask and there was a hard collar around his neck. A small portable monitor blipped away next to his head.

Hamish nodded at a crew who were waiting to whisk his current patient away. 'Thanks,' he said as they snapped up the rails of the gurney and pushed the patient briskly towards the waiting ambulance.

He turned his attention to the new patient. 'He's breathing,' the female officer continued as if she hadn't stopped. 'His pulse is fifty-eight but he's unconscious, sats are good.'

Hamish didn't like the pulse being that low—it should be rattling along, working overtime to compensate for the trauma his body had sustained.

'He was right at the bottom of the collapsed balcony debris.'

The guy looked remarkably untouched, considering, but Hamish had been doing this long enough to know that sometimes it was the way of things. That internal injuries weren't visible from the outside.

He pulled off his gloves and grabbed a new pair from the box in his bag and snapped them on. The bag was somewhat depleted now. He crouched then knelt against the rough bitumen yet again. His knees protested the move but Hamish ignored the pain. Gravel rash was a minor inconvenience compared to burns, blast injuries and the other trauma he'd seen in the last few hours.

'Do you know his name?' So many of the victims hadn't had an ID on them but Hamish always liked to know who he was treating.

'Wesley, according to the driver's licence in the wallet we found in his pocket.'

Hamish nodded. 'Thanks.' The rescue squad officers turned to go. 'How many fatalities?' His voice was quiet but enough to stop the woman in her tracks. He'd been trying not to notice the line of bodies beneath the sheets growing but every time he lifted his head they were in his line of sight.

'Twenty-six.'

He shut his eyes briefly, the image of a purple dress fluttering through his mind like the sails of a kite. It was going to be a really terrible Christmas for a lot of families across the city.

'Wesley.' Hamish turned to his patient, his voice deep and authoritative as he delivered a brisk sternal rub.

Nothing.

'Wesley,' he said again, deeper and a little louder as he shone his penlight into the patient's eyes. Both were fixed and dilated. Neither responded to light.

Oh, no. Crap.

Jenny crouched beside him. 'Bad?'

Hamish nodded. 'Non-responsive. Pupils fixed, dilated. GCS of three.'

'Okay, then.' Jenny grabbed her bag. 'Let's intubate, get some lines in and get him to hospital. This guy has a date with a neurosurgeon's drill.'

Hamish didn't think Jenny really believed performing a burr hole was going to result in a positive outcome. They had no idea how long Wesley had been in this condition. If he'd had surgery performed immediately post-injury, it *might* have helped, but it was probably way too late by now.

More likely the sustained pressure in his head from a bleed, which had probably occurred when his skull had crashed into the ground, had caused diffuse injury. If he came though this, the likelihood of a severe neurological deficit was strong.

But one thing he knew for sure was that sometimes people surprised you and it wasn't their job to make ethical decisions. It was their job to save who could be saved and Wesley had made it thus far. And, hell, Hamish wanted to believe that a guy who was still breathing, despite the trauma he'd received, could pull through this.

God knew, they needed a Christmas miracle after everything tonight.

* * *

Lola wasn't surprised to see Hamish pushing through the swing doors of her intensive care unit. Normally paramedics dropped patients in the emergency department and Emergency brought them to ICU if warranted. But when a patient was already intubated it saved time and handling for paramedics to bring the patient directly to ICU. They'd had two admissions like this already tonight from the night club bombing.

She was pleased it was him accompanying the patient this time, though. She'd figured he'd be there on scene somewhere and she hadn't realised how tense she'd been about it until she'd spotted him and the grimness of his mouth had kicked up into a familiar smile.

It wasn't that she thought Hamish might be in some kind of danger, it was more professional empathy. Lola could only guess at the kind of carnage he must have witnessed from what had already come in here and from the news reports they were hearing. Dozens of crushed, broken and burned bodies. Bright young things just out having fun. And so close to Christmas.

Things like that could do a number on your head.

'Bed twelve,' she said.

As one of the shifts runners, it had been Lola's job to get the bed space ready for their new admission. They'd been alerted to this arrival about fifteen minutes ago so she'd had time to customise the set-up for a patient with a head injury. And now it was action stations as two more nurses—the one assigned to look after Wesley and the nurse in charge—and two doctors—the ICU and the neuro registrar—descended on bed twelve.

They worked as a team, listening to Hamish's methodical handover as they got Wesley on the bed, hooked him up to the ventilator, plugged him into the monitors, started up some fluids and commenced some sedation.

The ICU registrar was inserting an arterial line as Hamish's handover drew to a close. By the time he'd answered all the questions that had been thrown at him, the arterial line was in, they had a red blood-pressure trace on the screen with an alarmingly wide pulse pressure and the registrar had thrust a full arterial blood gas syringe at Lola and she filled some lab tubes with blood from another syringe.

'Go and get some coffee,' she threw over her shoulder to Hamish and Jenny as she headed for the blood gas machine out back. Jenny knew where the staffroom was and they looked like they could do with some bolstering.

Lola was inserting the blood-filled syringe into the machine when Hamish appeared and said, 'Hey.'

He reeked of smoke and looked like hell. 'Hey.' She smiled at him for a beat or two, her heart squeezing, before she returned her attention to entering Wesley's details into the computer.

He didn't say anything, just watched her, and she waited for the machine to beep at her to remove the syringe before she said anything. 'Are you okay?' she asked.

It would take a couple of minutes for the machine to print out the results so she had the time to check up on him.

'Yep.' His smile warmed his eyes and was immensely reassuring. 'Just tired.'

She nodded. 'How was it out there?'

He didn't say anything for a moment then shook his head. 'Awful.'

Lola didn't have any reply to that. No easy words to soothe the terrible memories no doubt still fresh in his mind. So she did the only thing she knew how to do, what nurses always did—she touched him. She reached across and squeezed his arm.

'Go.' She squeezed his arm again. 'Get coffee. I think there's still some choc-chip biscuits someone brought in earlier too. You look like you need a sugar hit.'

He gave a half-laugh that sounded so weary she wanted to tuck him into bed herself. 'You look tired too.'

That was an understatement. It was almost six and Lola hadn't even had a break yet. Not even to go to the bathroom. She wasn't tired mentally, but physically she was exhausted. Her feet throbbed, her lower back twinged, her stomach growled and she had a dull ache behind her eyes.

Being a runner usually meant a busy shift but some shifts were crazily busy. Like tonight with their third critical admission as well as several existing patients who'd decided tonight was the night to destabilise.

Emma was one of them.

Her blood pressure had shot up at the start of the shift and it'd taken them several worrying hours to get it down to a much safer reading. She was fine again now but it was just further evidence of the instability of her failing heart. A transplant couldn't happen soon enough.

Lola shrugged off her weariness. It was just the way it went sometimes. 'It's almost knock-off time.' That was the one consolation. In an hour and a half her shift would be over—so would his—and they could both get some well-earned sleep.

The blood-gas machine spewed out a strip of paper, which Lola tore off and studied. 'How is it?' Hamish asked.

'Not great.' She handed it to him. 'His carbon dioxide level's too high.' Which would increase his intracranial pressure—not the thing Wesley's brain needed.

'I've got to get this back to the reg.' He nodded and handed the slip over, stepping away from the doorway so she could pass. He fell in beside her as she walked briskly to the bed space. 'I'll probably be late home,' she said. 'This place is a mess and we're not going to get a chance to play catch-up until the morning staff come on.'

There was a roomful of discarded equipment out back that needed attention and things were in desperate need of a restock.

'I don't think I'm going to be home early either. Jenny mentioned something about the boss probably wanting to do a bit of an informal debrief with her before we leave so...'

Lola nodded. 'Good idea.' She pulled up beside the registrar and handed over the blood-gas printout. 'Now go get coffee.'

He smiled. 'Yes ma'am.'

CHAPTER NINE

LOLA HAD NOT long succumbed to sleep on the couch when the door opened and her eyelids pinged open. Between the hurricane-like roar of the fan overhead and the fact that she'd dropped like a stone into the deepest depths of unconsciousness, she was amazed she'd heard a thing.

She must have really been attuned to the key in the lock!

Squinting at the time on the television display—it was almost ten—she swung her legs to the floor. 'Hamish?'

'Sorry,' he said from somewhere behind her. 'I didn't mean to wake you. I thought you'd be in bed. What are you doing out here?'

Lola's thoughts floated in a thick soup of disorientation. What *was* she doing out here? 'I'm…waiting for you to come home.'

'Sorry, I didn't realise. Debrief went on for ever.'

He appeared in front of her, lowering himself down on the end of the coffee table and setting his backpack on the floor. There were a few feet separating them but, as always, she felt the tug of him.

'You didn't have to wait up.'

Lola shrugged. Did he think she'd just go to bed after the things he'd seen last night without checking in with him first? Just because she didn't think they should get intimately involved, it didn't mean they still couldn't care for each other, have empathy for each other.

'It's fine,' she dismissed, suddenly realising that he was in shorts and T-shirt instead of his uniform and that his russet hair was damp and curling at his nape. 'You had a shower at work?' He didn't usually.

'Yeah. Everything stank of smoke, even my hair.'

He ran his palms down his thighs, drawing her gaze to the gold-blond hairs on his legs and the state of his knees. They were crisscrossed with tiny livid cuts and areas that had been rubbed raw.

'Do they hurt?'

'A little.' He shrugged as if it was just a mild inconvenience. 'How's Wesley?'

Lola had been waiting for the question, knowing it would come. She wished she had better news to tell Hamish, even though she knew *he* knew full well the severity of Wesley's injuries. 'He'd not long come back from CT when I left.'

He nodded slowly. 'Bad?'

'Diffuse brain injury with severe cerebral swelling. They were prepping him for Theatre.'

'Right.' He nodded and rose from the table, heading to the kitchen. She heard the fridge door open and he called, 'You want a beer?'

'No.' Lola didn't think twice at Hamish consuming a beer at ten in the morning. Quite a few of her colleagues had a drink or two before going to sleep after night duty. They swore it was better than sleeping tablets, which many shift workers resorted to.

He reappeared in the kitchen doorway, leaning against the jamb as he took a few deep swallows. The hem of his T-shirt lifted slightly, flashing a strip of tanned abs.

'They're saying on television that the bomb was set off by some guy who's a disgruntled ex-employee,' she said.

'Yeah, I heard. Death toll's risen to thirty-four too.' He wandered closer as if he was going to resume his seat on the table but changed course, heading for the balcony, stopping short to just stare out the door she'd opened earlier.

Lola didn't say anything, waiting for him to

say more. If he wanted to. When he didn't, she filled the silence. 'You want to talk about it?'

He shook his head. 'Nope.' But within a few seconds he was turning around, his eyes seeking hers, searching hers. 'I've been trying to wrap my head around how that guy justified this to himself.' He took a swig of his beer. 'I mean, you got sacked, dude. I get it. That sucks.' He shrugged. 'Rant at your boss or your wife, go home and kick the wall. But *why* would anyone think it's okay to seek revenge like this? To kill so many innocent people?'

Lola shook her head. 'I…don't know.' She wished she did. She wished she had the answers he sought.

He was obviously still in the thick of the action inside his head. Probably second-guessing his every move, wishing he'd done something differently. That stuff took time to fully tease out. Took a lot of reflection before a person came to the conclusion that they'd done the best they could.

'I don't know why some people do terrible things, Hamish, but thank goodness for people like you.' She smiled at him because he looked so lonely all the way over there by himself. 'For those who charge in to help when everyone else is running away. There'd be a lot more fatalities from last night without people like you around.'

He nodded. 'Yeah.' Tipping his head back, he drained his beer, staring at the bottle in his hands for a moment or two before he glanced at her and said, 'Think I'll hit the sack now.'

'You should. You look dead on your feet.' He was swaying and his eyes were bloodshot. She'd bet her last cent they were as gritty as hers. There were tiny lines around his eyes that she'd never noticed before and his impossibly square jaw was as tight as a steel trap.

'Says the woman with a cushion mark on her face and scary hair.'

Lola gaped for a moment before his lips spread into a smile and a low chuckle slipped from his mouth. She pushed her hands through her fuzzy mane to tame the knotty, blonde ringlets but there was no nope for them. She probably looked like she'd been pulled through a hedge backwards, while he looked good enough to eat.

Even exhausted, the man wore sexy better than any man had a right to.

'Your sense of humour's pretty tired too, I see.'

'Yep.' He grinned. 'We're both kinda beat.'

'At least you only have one more night. I have three.' Lola didn't mind night shift but when the unit was busy for a sustained period of time like it had been, a run of night shifts could really take it out of her.

'Some days off would be good,' Hamish said, cutting into her thoughts.

Yeah. He could no doubt use some mental time-out after last night. But, more than anything, right now he needed to sleep.

They both did.

'Okay, well, I'm taking my scary hair to bed.' It didn't seem like he was going to make the first move towards the bedrooms so she did it for him. 'Night-night.'

She didn't look at him as she turned away in case she did something crazy like offer to rock him to sleep. She just kept walking until she pulled her door shut, placing temptation firmly on the other side.

Hamish woke at two in the afternoon for about the tenth time. His room was on the side of the apartment that copped full sunlight for most of the day, and the curtains at the big window wouldn't block out candlelight, let alone the December sun in Sydney. It hadn't ever bothered him before and he could usually sleep like the dead after night shift.

But he hadn't just been through a normal night shift.

He was coming off an adrenaline high that

had left him wrung out and edgy, his brain grappling with the images of the kids he'd helped and all those bodies under sheets. When he did manage to drift off, his dreams were haunted by a woman in a purple dress.

Just like he'd known they would be.

And now he was awake again. Exhausted, but too chicken to close his eyes, plus it was too hot to fall asleep, anyway. There was sweat on his chest and in the small of his back. The fan going at full speed did nothing but push the stifling air around.

He *had* to sleep. He *needed* to sleep. He had to operate a vehicle in six hours *and* be thinking clearly. He wouldn't be any help to anyone if he went to work even more exhausted than he'd left it.

Hamish rolled on his side, forced himself to shut his eyes, to breathe in through his nose and out through his mouth. To do it again and again until he started to drift. And then a flutter of purple fabric splattered in blood billowed through his mind and his eyes flicked open.

Grabbing his pillows, he plonked them on top of his head, shoved his face into them and let out a giant *yawp!*

'Hamish?'

Startled, he ripped the pillows off his head to find Lola striding into his room, her short gown covering her from neck to knee but hugging everything in between. He was pretty sure she wasn't wearing much of anything underneath.

Great.

'Lola?'

'Are you okay?' She stood at the end of the bed, her forehead creased, her arms folded tight against her chest.

'Yes.' Hamish flopped onto his back and stared at the ceiling. It was that or ogle her. 'Just…can't sleep. Have you been skulking outside my door?'

'No.' He smiled at the affront in her voice. 'I was just passing to get a drink of water and I heard a noise. I thought you were…upset or something.'

He gave a harsh laugh, air huffing from his lungs. *Great.* Lola thought he was lying in bed, crying. It'd be emasculating if he wasn't currently sporting an erection the size of the Opera House.

He thanked God for his decision to keep his underwear on today and for the sheet that was bunched over his crotch.

'I'm frustrated,' he told the ceiling. *In more ways than one*. 'I need to sleep but my brain is ticking over and the fan is totally useless in this heat.' He raised his head again. 'We even have air-con in the country, Lola, what gives?'

'Grace and I moved into the apartment in the middle of winter. And there were fans... they're usually enough.'

'How do you sleep after nights on days like this?'

'Well, my room is quite a bit cooler than yours. Grace said I should take it because she didn't work nights on her job. But I have been known to get up and walk through a cold shower then flop on the bed wringing wet and let the fan air-dry me. That's almost as good as air-con.'

Hamish shut his eyes and suppressed a rising groan as his head fell back against the pillow. That image was not helping the situation in his underwear. Not one little bit.

'Are you dreaming about it?'

About her being wet and naked on her bed? He sure as hell would be now. But he knew that wasn't what she was talking about. He sighed. 'Yes.'

'You want to talk about it?'

'No.' What he wanted was to drag her down on the bed, rip that gown off her, roll her under him and sink inside her, and just forget about it all for a while. 'I don't want to talk about it. I don't even want to *think* about it. What I want right now is to just forget it so I can get to sleep. I *need* to sleep. I want it to *not* be forty degrees in this room so I can just *go to sleep*.'

She didn't say anything for a long time and a weird kind of tension built in his abdomen. Hamish lifted his head and immediately wished he hadn't. The way she was looking at him shot sparks right up his spine.

'What?' His voice was annoyingly raspy and he cleared it as her gaze roved over his body.

She nodded then, as if to herself, before saying, 'I can help you with that.'

Hamish swore he could feel his heart skip a beat. Where the hell was she going with this? Was she going to fix him a long cool drink or was she offering something else? 'What do you suggest?'

'My room is cooler and sex is not only the best sleeping pill around but I've generally found that if it's good enough it can also induce a temporary kind of amnesia. I can only surmise from the kind of sex we've already had together that the amnesia will be significant. What do you think?'

Hamish blinked. What didn't he think? There was no hope for his erection now.

He should decline. It was all kinds of screwed up and he knew how it'd mess with the boundaries they'd put in place. But he'd be lying if he

said he didn't crave the solace—the oblivion—
she was offering.

Didn't crave the white noise of pleasure, her
breathy pants, the way she called his name as
she came. Didn't crave the company of another
human being, someone to hold onto in a world
that seemed a little less shiny than it had yesterday.

Someone he wanted more than he'd ever
wanted anyone. His heart rattled in his chest
just thinking about being with Lola again.

'Please, Hamish.' She took a step forward,
her features earnest. She'd obviously taken his
silence as a pending *no* instead of a considered *hell, yes*. 'I know we said we shouldn't do
this and we've both been trying to respect that.
But…our jobs are… There's a lot of emotional
pressure and sometimes we need an outlet. Let
me do this for you. Let me be there for you the
way you were there for me that night when I
needed comfort and distraction. Unless you're
too tired?'

Hamish gave a half laugh, half snort. 'Too
tired for sex?'

She shrugged. 'I heard that's a thing.'

He grabbed the sheet bunched at his hips and
threw it back to reveal how *not* tired he was.
'It's not a thing for me.'

Her eyes zeroed in on his underwear, following the ridge of his erection, and Hamish felt it as potently as if it had been her tongue. Her gaze drifted down a little then back up again, finally settling between his legs.

'So I see.' She dragged her attention back to his face and held out her hand. 'What are we waiting for?'

Hamish didn't have a clue. He vaulted upright, swung his legs out of the bed and rose to his feet, reaching for her hand. His pulse raced now as they headed across the hallway. The last time they'd done this it'd been the middle of the night. It'd been unexpected, spontaneous. There'd been haste, urgency. They'd groped blindly, they'd fumbled.

This was broad daylight, and premeditated.

She opened her door and led him inside where the heavy blinds at the window blocked out the light and the sparseness of the furniture and walls made it feel cave-like. And with the fan on high speed the temperature *was* several degrees lower. It wasn't cool exactly but the edge had been taken off the heat.

'Bloody hell,' he grumbled. 'I've been sweltering out there in the desert while you've been hibernating in a cave.'

She laughed and her hand slipped from his

as she moved towards the bed. 'I thought you country boys could handle the heat.'

'What can I say? You've already made a pampered city slicker out of me.'

'*That* I find hard to believe.'

Hamish smiled as he watched her open a bedside drawer and bend over it slightly as she fished around inside. The gown rose nicely up the backs of her thighs and he didn't even bother to pretend he wasn't checking out her ass.

She found what she wanted and turned to face him, brandishing a square foil packet in the air for a second before tossing it on the bed. Then, as he watched, she tugged on the tie at her waist holding her gown in place. It fell open, revealing a swathe of skin right down her middle. The two inner swells of her breasts, her stomach, some lacy underwear and upper thighs. His mouth turned as dry as the dust in the cattle yards back home.

She smiled. 'You want to come a little closer?'

Hamish did, he really did. He strode over, his heart in his mouth as he stopped close enough to slip a hand inside her gown if he wanted. And he wanted. But he wanted to kiss her more. He wanted to kiss her until they both couldn't breathe.

He placed his hands on her face, cradling her cheeks, his eyes searching hers, looking for pity and finding only the softness of empathy. And a glitter of lust. He brushed a thumb over her lips and she made a noise at the back of her throat as she parted her lips. The breeze from the fan blew a curl from her temple across her face and he hooked it back with his index finger.

'You're so beautiful,' he whispered as he slowly lowered his mouth to hers.

Their lips met and her soft moan was like a hit of adrenaline to his system, tripping through his veins, whooshing through his lungs, taking the kiss from a light touch to a long, drugging exploration that left them both breathless and needy.

When he pulled back her lips were full and wet from his kisses and a deep reddish-pink. She looked like she'd been thoroughly kissed and damn if being the one to put *that* look on her face wasn't a huge turn-on. His hands slid to her shoulders, his thumbs hooking into the open lapels of her gown, which he slowly pushed back. The gown skimmed the tops of her shoulders before sliding down her arms, and falling off to pool at her feet.

Hamish sucked in a breath at the roundness

of her breasts, at the light pink circle of her areolas and the way the nipples beaded despite the heat. His hands brushed from her neck to the slopes of her breasts, trailing down to the very tips before palming them, filling his hands with their fullness.

'Hamish.' Her voice was a breathy whisper and she swayed a little and shut her eyes as he kissed her again. Kissed her as he stroked and kneaded her breasts, kissed her until she was moaning and arching her back, her thighs pressed to his.

His hands slid lower, skimming her ribs and her hips, using his thumbs once again as a hook to remove her underwear, breaking off the kiss as he slid them down, crouching before her to pull them all the way down her legs. He looked up as she stepped out of them and her hands slid into his hair and he dropped a kiss on the top of each thigh, his nostrils filling with the heady scent of her arousal.

Hamish kissed his way back up, brushing his lips against her hip bone and her belly button and the underside of each breast and the centre of her chest and her neck then back to her mouth, groaning as she slid her arms around his neck and smooshed her naked body along the length of his, grinding her pelvis into him.

'Mmm…' he murmured against her mouth, his hands tightening on her ass. 'That feels good.'

'It'd feel better if you were naked too,' she said, her voice husky.

Hamish didn't need to be told twice and quickly pulled off his own underwear to stand in front of her naked, his erection standing thick and proud between them.

'Oh, yes,' she whispered, her hand reaching out to stroke him. 'Much better.'

Hamish shut his eyes as she petted him, her fingers trailing up and down his shaft, the muscles in his ass tensing uncontrollably, electricity buzzing low in his spine, his heart thumping like a gong in his chest.

Her fingers grew bolder, sliding around him, and he groaned again as he opened his eyes. 'Enough.' He grabbed her hand. 'I'm not sure how long I'm going to last and I want to be inside you.'

'God… Yes, please.'

Hamish lowered himself onto the bed and pulled her down on top of him, revelling in the easy way she straddled him, in the way his erection slid through the slickness between her legs, in the way she grabbed the condom and sheathed him, in the way her breasts swung and she moaned as he touched them, in the way her blonde curls blew around her head as she looked down at him.

His hands tightened on her hips. She was magnificent on top of him, so comfortable with her nudity and taking charge. She lifted her hips and took him in hand, notching his erection at her entrance, closing her eyes to enjoy the feel of it for a moment.

She took his breath away. 'You look like a goddess.'

She opened her eyes and smiled. 'You can call me Aphrodite.' And she lowered herself onto him.

Hamish groaned, watching her as he sank to the hilt inside her, watching pleasure spread over her face and satisfaction take over as she settled on him, her bottom lip caught between her teeth.

'Oh, yes,' she whispered, raising her arms above her head and sinking her hands into her hair, her breasts thrusting, her back arching.

She was gloriously unrestrained and she was his.

'*Now* you're Aphrodite.'

He moved then and she moved with him, her hands still in her hair, rocking her hips, undulating her stomach, riding him like a belly dancer, taking his thrusts, absorbing them, consumed in the rocking and the pounding,

building her, building him—building them—
to fever point, the frantic whistle of the fan a
back note to the wild tango between them.

Hamish's climax gathered speed and light
and momentum, little daggers of pleasure bur-
rowing into his backside, the tension in his
stomach and groin starting to unravel, and he
could almost reach out and touch the rapture.
He slid his fingers between her legs, wanting
her there with him, *needing* her there.

She moaned as he found the hard knot of
her clitoris and she gasped as he squeezed
it, the sensation jolting like a shock through
her body, her internal muscles clamping hard
around him.

'Hamish!'

She sobbed his name as the rapture took her,
and he cried out to her too, as it collected him,
his fingers digging into her hips as his spine
electrified and his seed surged from his body.
He pulsed inside her and she pulsed around
him, the pleasure sweeping them along, ravag-
ing them, their movements jerky, their dance
disorganised, neither of them caring as they
rode the rapture right to the very end.

It lifted as dramatically as it had descended,
Lola collapsing against him, her curls spilling
over his chest as she gasped for breath. She
was hot against him but he didn't care. He was

burning up too and moisture slicked between their bodies, but all that mattered was that they were burning up together.

She rolled off him eventually and Hamish groaned as he slid from her body. He turned his head to watch her. She looked utterly sated, a satisfied tilt to her lips. There was a line of sweat on her upper lip as well as on her forehead and her chest and in the hollow at the base of her throat.

'So that first time wasn't a fluke, then?' she said, slurring her words a little, obviously sleepy.

Hamish chuckled. 'Nope.'

He assumed she knew how special that was. To be so *simpatico* with another person? To feel as if you *fitted* together. As if you were their *perfect fit*. He'd never felt it with another woman.

He shut his eyes, enjoying the thought and the coolness of the air from the fan drying his sweat and the stillness in his head, surrendering for a second or two to the tug of exhaustion, before rousing to dispose of the condom. Lola was already asleep, her body rosy from their contact, her blonde curls frothing around her head, a small smile still touching her mouth.

He crawled back in beside her—it never occurred to him to return to his own bed. Not now. This might only be a one-off but he was going to hold onto it for as long as he could.

He was going to lie down beside her and sleep—wonderful, wonderful sleep—and he was going to worry about the rest later.

CHAPTER TEN

ON HER LAST night shift, Lola was assigned to Emma who, although stable, still desperately needed a heart transplant. She'd been listed for almost six weeks now, which was truly pushing it, and there *would* come a point where Emma started to decompensate, despite medical technology's best efforts to keep her stable.

Then she'd be just another *died on the waiting list* statistic.

Which was tragic at any age but at twenty-three it was just too awful to contemplate.

Despite the underlying desperation of the situation, Emma was chugging along and Lola found her mind drifting back to Hamish. In her bed. They'd slept together three days in a row and she was counting on making that a fourth.

They hadn't talked about what had happened between them that morning after the bombing. Lola had just *understood* what he'd needed and hadn't been able to deny him. Not when he'd been *her* comfort, *her* solace, *her* soft place to land that first night they'd spent together all those months ago.

And she'd wanted to be that person for him.

They hadn't discussed sleeping together again either. When she'd made the offer, it had been a one-time-only kind of thing.

The rest had just kind of happened.

They'd arrived home that next morning at the same time and it had seemed like the most natural thing in the world for her to join him in the shower, to soap him up, lay her hands on him, her mouth on him, until he had her up against the tiles, driving into her, withdrawing as he came because neither of them had thought about their lack of protection when things had started to get handsy.

And then he'd carried her through to her bed, both of them still wet, and they'd drifted off, their skin cooling under the roar of the fan, her heart happy. They'd woken twice during the day to join again, half-asleep but reaching for each other despite the fact she had to work that night.

Lola wasn't used to being gripped by such… attraction. Sure, she'd been with good-looking men, but she didn't need a *hubba-hubba* reaction to a guy to go to bed with him and sex had just been an itch to scratch. A fun but necessary biological function.

But these last few days had blown that theory out of the water. There was sex, there was *good* sex and there was *whoa Nelly!* sex. She'd had some of the first, quite a bit of the second but never any of the third. Until Hamish. He was the whole package—physically attractive and a magician between the sheets—and it had been totally consuming.

'Hey.'

Lola glanced up after finishing a suction of Emma's tracheostomy tube—a breathing tube had been inserted into her neck a few weeks ago—to find Grace approaching. She'd been here when Lola had arrived on shift but it didn't stop the spurt of guilt Lola felt every time she saw her friend, especially given the direction of her thoughts.

'Hey.'

Heat crept into Lola's cheeks despite telling herself she'd done nothing wrong. Hamish was an adult. He didn't have to check it was okay with his sister to sleep with Lola and Grace had already dismissed those concerns anyway. But, deep down, Lola knew that Grace would want to know.

It might not be one of the Ten Commandments but *Thou shall not sleep with your best friend's brother without at least giving her all the gory details* was ingrained in the female psyche.

Lola thanked God for the low lighting Emma's stable condition allowed at the bed space and smiled, determined to act normal, even if she did feel like she was wearing an 'I'm sleeping with your brother' sign around her neck.

'How are you?' Lola asked.

It wasn't a standard throw-away question. It was a genuine enquiry about what Grace was dealing with tonight. Just prior to Lola commencing, Wesley, who hadn't recovered or responded in the seventy-two hours since the bombing of the nightclub, had undergone his second set of neurological function tests and been declared brain-dead.

It was a tragic end to such a young life and had raised the death toll from the bombing to thirty-five. The one glimmer of hope from the situation was Wesley's parents, who had generously and selflessly consented for his organs to be donated.

And it was Grace's job to co-ordinate everything. Which was a massive undertaking. Everything from ensuring all the correct tests were done and protocols followed, to liaising with other teams and hospitals involved with the recipients, to choreographing the harvesting that was going to occur in a few hours, to being there for Wesley's family fell under Grace's purview in this instance.

'Are you okay?' Lola pressed.

She knew how difficult these cases were to deal with. How talking with bewildered and bereaved people looking for answers you couldn't give them was emotionally sapping. How being strong for them required superhuman levels of empathy and patience and gentleness and sometimes meant bearing the brunt of their grief and anger.

Just watching Wesley's distraught family as they came and went from his bedside had taken a little piece of Lola's heart. It was simply heartbreaking to watch and there wasn't one nurse on the unit tonight who wasn't affected by it.

Grace grimaced. 'I'm okay.'

A silent moment passed between them. An acknowledgment that the situation sucked, that Wesley's death was a tragedy about to spawn a lot of happy endings for people staring down the barrels of their own tragedies.

Organ transplantation was truly a double-edged sword.

Lola stripped her gloves off. 'Everything sorted now?'

Grace gave a half-laugh that told Lola she

wasn't getting home to Marcus any time soon. 'Things are coming together,' she said, obviously downplaying how much still had to be put in place.

It didn't fool Lola an iota.

'But I do have some good news.' She tipped her head to the side to indicate Lola should meet her at the bottom of the bed.

Lola removed her protective eyewear and washed her hands at the nearby basin before joining her friend at the computer station at the end of Emma's bed. 'I thought you might like to be the first to know,' Grace said, her voice low. 'Emma's a match for Wesley's heart.'

Lola stared at Grace incredulously for a moment. The possibility had been in the back of her mind but she'd dismissed it as being highly unlikely. Lola *had* seen it once before a few years back when the donor and a recipient had been on the unit together but it wasn't common.

'Really?'

Grace beamed. 'Really. They're ringing Emma's parents now.'

Lola's heart just about grew wings and lifted out of her chest. It was a moment of indescribable joy. *Emma was getting a new heart.* The backs of Lola's eyes pricked with moisture and her arms broke out in goose-bumps.

'That's…*wonderful* news.'

Grace nodded. 'Right? It's nice in this job when you get to give happy news.'

Lola gave her friend a hug because she was overjoyed but also because Grace probably needed it after all she'd been dealing with. Of course, it didn't take long for the logistics to dawn. To know that her night was suddenly going to get a lot busier, following all the pre-donation protocols and getting Emma ready for the operating theatre.

But the realisation that a usually anonymous process might not stay that way dawned the heaviest.

The truth of the matter was that families of ICU patients talked to each other. The unit had a very comfortable, well-equipped relatives' room, where people hung out. And talked. They talked about their loved ones—about the ups and downs, about the good days and the bad days, about the improvements and the setbacks.

Often they became *very* close, particularly in long-term cases like Emma's.

But donation was supposed to be anonymous. In most cases, donor families never met recipients. Usually about six weeks after the patient had died and their organs had been transplanted, the donor family was written to and given some basic information about the recipients in very generic detail.

Like, the right kidney went to a fifty-eight-year-old male who had been on the waiting list for ten years. Or the left lobe of the liver went to an eighteen-month-old baby girl and the remaining lobes were transplanted into to a thirty-one-year-old father of three.

But never names. Identities were always kept confidential. The whole process was ruled by a protocol of ethics and anonymity was strictly adhered to. It was too potentially fraught otherwise for recipients if donor families knew their names and where they lived. Also fraught for donor families.

If a recipient died due to complications after transplant—which did happen—what extra burden of grief could that put on already fragile families?

Organ donation was the ultimate altruistic gift and the lynchpin of that was anonymity.

Except now there were two families in the relatives' room—one whose son was brain-dead and about to have his organs harvested and the other whose daughter was about to get a heart transplant.

It wasn't going to take great powers of deduction to figure out the link.

'Have Wesley's family been interacting much with Emma's family?' Lola asked.

'Apparently not. They're still in that numbed, shocked stage and have kept to themselves. And Emma's family are down the coast for the night at some family thing so hopefully Wesley will be gone from the unit by the time Emma's family arrives back.'

'Fingers crossed we'll get lucky and neither will figure it out.' The other time it had happened, they'd managed to maintain the anonymity of the process. It had been touch and go for a moment but it had all worked out in the end. 'Are they going to use the Reflections Suite?'

Reflections was a self-contained unit two floors up that families of deceased patients could use to spend time saying goodbye to their loved ones, in private, before they were taken to the morgue. It was roomy with comfy chairs and couches and a kitchenette with a fridge. They were able to take all the time they needed to grieve as a family and be together in their loss.

Grace nodded. 'Yes. I'll go up with Wesley to the suite after the operation is finished and sit with the family for a bit if they want.'

Lola nodded. Grace was going to have a long, emotionally challenging night. 'Isn't that what the on-call social worker is for?'

'He'll be available to them too. But it's me they've been dealing with through this process so…' Grace shrugged. 'I want them to have some continuity and be able to answer any lingering questions they might have.'

'Yeah.' Lola nodded.

Caring for ICU patients meant caring for their families as well. And continuity, especially in acute situations, made everything much easier for grieving families.

Grace's pager went off and she pulled it off her belt, reading the message quickly. 'That's the Adelaide co-ordinator. Gotta go.'

Lola smiled. 'Of course. Go. I'll see you later.'

Grace darted off and Lola glanced at Emma and smiled before getting back to work. It was going to be another long night.

Lola was mentally exhausted as she entered the apartment eight hours later but her body was buzzing. In just a few days it had become scarily accustomed to Hamish being there and this morning was no different. In fact, it was probably worse.

They'd relaxed the rules about their roomie-only relationship and her cravings were growing.

Not even the prospect of telling him about

Wesley's death seemed to put a lid on the hum in her cells. Lola knew Hamish was holding out hope that Wesley might make some kind of meaningful recovery, even though the news had been dire since the beginning. Hamish had asked after him every morning and Lola had filled him in on what she knew.

She doubted Wesley's death would come as much of a surprise but it would no doubt take a piece of Hamish's heart as it had taken a piece of hers.

'Hey, you.'

Lordy, he was a sight for sore eyes, lounging against the kitchen benchtop, a carton of orange juice in his hand. Her breath hitched as she pulled up in the doorway. He'd obviously just had a shower as his hair was damp and all that covered him was a towel slung low on his hips. His chest and abs were smooth and bare, his stomach muscles arrowing down nicely to the knot in the towel.

'I was hoping you'd still be in bed.'

He gave a nonchalant shrug but ruined it with a wicked grin. 'I've been for a run.'

'Of course you have.'

Lola laughed, feeling like an absolute sloth in his presence as she walked straight into his arms. His hands moved to the small of her back as hers slid up and over his shoulders on their way to his neck, revelling in the warm flesh and the taut stretch of his skin over rounded joints and firm muscles.

She sighed, grateful that the temperature had eased yesterday afternoon and she could get this close and personal without being a ball of sweat in five seconds flat. She pressed her cheek against a bare pec, the steady thump of his heartbeat both reassuring and thrilling. When he tried to break the embrace she held on harder.

'Lola? Everything okay?'

She could hear the frown in his voice and she pulled away slightly, gazing up into his face. His face did funny things to her equilibrium. How had his face come to mean so much to her in such a short time?

'Lola?' His hands slid to her arms and gave a gentle squeeze. 'What?'

Even with his brow creased in concern, his blue eyes earnest, she wanted to lick his mouth. 'It's Wesley.'

He didn't say anything for a moment but she was aware the second he knew what she was about to say. 'Oh.'

Lola stroked her fingers along the russet stubble decorating his jaw line. 'He was declared brain dead just before I started last night.'

'Yeah.' Hamish nodded. 'Guess that was inevitable.'

'Doesn't make it suck any less.'

He gave a half-laugh. 'No.'

Lola cuddled into him again, her cheek to his pec, hoping her body against his would be some kind of comfort. His arms came around her as he rested his chin on the top of her head.

'He'd be a suitable donor, right? Did his family consent?'

'Yes.' Lola broke away to look at him.

'Yeah?' Hamish brightened. 'That's fantastic.'

Lola beamed at him. She couldn't agree more. 'And guess what?'

He smiled. 'What?'

Strictly speaking, what she was about to tell him was breaking patient confidentiality, but healthcare professionals often did discuss patients past and present, particularly in overlapping cases where there'd been multi-team involvement, so Lola didn't have a problem divulging. And she figured Hamish would appreciate this particular silver lining.

'Guess who got his heart?'

He frowned for a moment but it cleared as quickly as it had formed. 'Your patient on the list?'

Lola nodded. 'She's in Theatre now.'

'Oh, God.' His smile almost split his face in two. 'That's…wonderful news.'

'The best.'

He kissed her then. Hard. And Lola melted the way she always did as her cares fell away and her body was consumed by the presence of *him*. His pine and coconut aroma fogged her senses. His touch dazzled and electrified everything in its path, drugging and energising in equal measure.

His fingers hummed at her nape, his lips buzzed against hers, the rough drag of his breath brushed like sandpaper over her skin. His heart thumped hard beneath her palm and the steel of his erection pressed into her belly.

She was so damn needy she wanted to simultaneously rub herself all over him *and* crawl inside him.

'Mmm…' He broke off and every nerve ending in Lola's body cried out at the loss. 'I missed you last night.'

Lola smiled. 'I have three days off now.'

He smiled back. 'Whatever shall we do?'

'Well…there is the Christmas shopping.'

'We *could* do that.'

Lola pretended to consider some more. 'We could take a drive along the northern beaches. Find a nice spot for a picnic?'

'Yep. We could definitely do that.' He ground

his erection into her belly. 'I was thinking of something a little more indoorsy.'

The delighted little moan that hovered in Lola's throat threatened to become full blown as Hamish adjusted the angle of their hips and the bulge behind the towel pressed against her in *all the right places*.

'Oh, yeah?' She shut her eyes at the mindless pleasure he could evoke with just a flex of his hips. 'What did you have in mind exactly?'

'Something that doesn't require clothes for the next three days would be awesome.'

Somewhere in the morass of her brain Lola knew she should reject his invitation. Try and pull things back now their night duty stint was over. She was already dangerously attached to Hamish—three days of naked time with him would only make this insane craving she had for him worse.

Oh, but she *wanted* him.

Wanted to spend three days talking and sleeping and kissing and getting to know each other *really* well.

Lola tossed caution to the wind. Hell, it was Christmas, right? She grinned at him as she grabbed for the knot sitting low between his hips. 'I think clothes are overrated.' She pulled it and the towel fell to the floor, the thickness of his erection jammed between them.

Oh, yes, that was better.

She glanced at it before returning her attention to Hamish's face. 'I need a shower. I'm having very dirty thoughts.'

'But I like it when you're filthy.'

Lola grinned, kissing him quickly before shimmying out of reach, her fingers going to the buttons of her work blouse, undoing them one by one as she walked slowly backwards, opening the shirt when she was done so he could get an eyeful of her blue lacy bra.

'Come and get me,' she murmured, before turning tail and sprinting to the bathroom, a large naked man hot on her heels.

CHAPTER ELEVEN

EMMA WAS STILL ventilated when Lola went back onto the early shift after her days off and wild horses wouldn't have stopped Lola from requesting her to look after.

To say Emma was markedly improved was a giant understatement. She was breathing for herself and almost weaned off the ventilator. Her blood pressure was good, her heart rate was excellent, all her blood tests were normal and there were no signs of rejection. All her drains were out and her exposed surgical incision was looking pink and healthy.

She'd come a long way in such a short time.

Her eyes lit up when Lola said hello first thing and she reached for Lola's hand and gave it a squeeze.

'She remembers you,' Barry said.

Lola smiled. She had looked after Emma a lot these past weeks. Had held her hand, talked to her, reassured her. But Emma had been very ill for most of it and the drugs she'd had on board had often caused memories to be jumbled. Lola wouldn't have been at all surprised had Emma not remembered anything or anyone.

In fact, given the long, intensive haul she'd been through, it was probably not a bad thing.

'You look amazing, Emma,' Lola said.

Emma smiled and pointed to her tracheostomy, mouthing, 'Out.' The position of the tube in her throat rendered her unable to vocalise.

Lola laughed. 'Hopefully today, yes. After the rounds this morning, okay?'

She rolled her eyes and kicked her feet a little to display her impatience. 'I know.' Lola squeezed her arm. 'Not much longer now, I promise.'

'I told you, Emsy,' Barry said, kissing her hand. 'Soon.'

Lola smiled. Barry had come a long way too.

'You think she'll be on a ward for Christmas?' Barry asked.

Lola shrugged. Christmas was still a week away. 'That's the way to bet. *But*—'

'Did you hear that?' Barry said, interrupting Lola to beam at Emma. The way he looked at her caught in Lola's throat. 'You'll be out of here soon.'

'*Maybe,*' Lola stressed. She didn't want to

rain on their parade but Lola had been doing this far too long not to be cautious about her predictions. 'Don't forget, it's one day at a time in here.

'We know, we know,' Barry said in a way that led Lola to believe they were already planning Emma's homecoming.

And Lola didn't have it in her to stop them. Inside Emma's chest beat Wesley's heart. His family's tragedy had become Emma's family's miracle and hell if Lola wasn't going to let them bask in that.

A few days before Christmas Hamish found himself sitting at the back of a packed cathedral in full uniform. He'd imagined a lot of different scenarios playing out during his urban stint in Sydney but attending a memorial service for the victims of a bombing had not been one of them.

Lola, one of the many hospital personnel in attendance, was by his side as the mayor talked about the tragic events that had unfolded that night and how the efforts of the emergency services had doubtless saved countless lives. He shifted uncomfortably in his seat, pulling the collar of his formal uniform shirt off his neck. It was stifling hot in the cavernous cathedral and praise such as this added to his discomfort.

He and everyone else who had attended that night and all the health care professionals who were caring for the injured—doctors and nurses like Lola and Grace—had just been doing their jobs.

Words like heroes and angels didn't sit well on his shoulders. He'd just done what he'd been paid to do.

A squeeze to his leg brought him out of his own head and he smiled at Lola, her hand a steadying presence spread over his thigh. He'd spent a lot of time in her arms avoiding thinking about the carnage of that night, but it was unavoidable today and he'd been discombobulated ever since meeting Wesley's parents earlier.

And somehow she knew it.

Jenny sat on his other side. She was rigid in her seat and tight-lipped, the buttons on her dress uniform as shiny as the tips of her black dress shoes. She shot him a small, strained smile as the minister at the front asked everyone to stand for the reading of the names.

They rose to their feet. Hamish knew how important these sorts of memorials were. That public grief, remembrance and acknowledgement brought communities together and paying respect helped people move on. He knew it would help him and Jenny move on from that night—eventually.

It still felt a little too raw right now, though, the girl in the purple dress still a little too fresh in his brain.

Abigail. That was her name. He'd seen it on TV.

Lola's hand slipped into his as the minister read the first name out and a candle was lit in their honour. He was so damn grateful to have her here. She'd become his distraction, his safe harbour, his soft place to land. She'd become vital—like oxygen and sunshine—and the thought of leaving her in a few weeks was like a knife to his heart.

Because he'd fallen in love with her.

The weird tension he'd been carrying in his shoulders for a while now eased at the realisation. If anything, it should have tightened because that was not part of *the plan*. Not that they'd talked about any plan. In fact, they'd studiously avoided it seeing that their last plan— to keep their hands off each other—obviously hadn't gone that well.

He should be worried. He should be grim. He should be nervous. Hell, he should at least be trying to figure it all out, work out his next step. But he was thirty years old and in love for the first time and right now, on this darkly emotional day, it was like a blast of light through the stained-glass windows of the cathedral.

It was enough.

The service ended fifteen minutes later and Hamish was finally able to breathe again. Jenny peeled off to talk to somebody she knew as they walked out into the fresh air and sunshine. Grace, who'd been up at the front supporting Wesley's family, waved and Lola's hand slipped from his as they headed in her direction.

Hamish missed the intimacy immediately and resentment stirred briefly in his chest before he got over himself. He didn't need Grace on his case as he tried to navigate this next couple of weeks. He kissed his sister on the cheek and she and Lola introduced the group of nurses they'd joined.

They made polite small talk for a few minutes but it was the last thing Hamish wanted to do. He wanted to be at home with Lola. He wanted to strip her out of her uniform and bury himself inside her and tell her with his body what he couldn't tell her with his words. Not yet anyway. Not until he'd figured out just how to do that without losing her in the process.

If that was even possible.

'You okay?' she asked, her voice low as the conversation ebbed and flowed around them.

Hamish nodded and smiled reassuringly. These people were clearly her work colleagues and friends and he needed to pull his head out from his ass. They'd all been part of the bombing and its aftermath in some way. 'Yes.'

'We'll, it's after twelve.' A male nurse who'd been introduced as Jay rubbed his hands together. 'Who's up for drinks at Billi's?'

There was a general murmur of, 'Count me in,' including from Grace and Lola.

'You, Hamish?' Jay asked.

Not really, no. He didn't want to go and psychoanalyse to death every part of that night, which was exactly what he knew would happen. It was inevitable when you got a bunch of health professionals together—it's what they did.

He just wanted to be alone with the woman he loved.

But Lola had already indicated she was going to the bar and he wanted to be wherever she was, even if it meant he couldn't touch her and he had to pretend everything was platonic between them. 'Um…sure.'

He glanced at Lola and smiled. But her eyes narrowed slightly and Hamish swore he could feel her probing his mind as she searched his face. 'Actually… I might take a rain-check.'

She turned back to Jay, the movement inching her closer to Hamish. He felt the slight brush of her arm against his, was conscious of their thighs almost touching.

'I still have some Christmas shopping to do and this is my only day off between now and Christmas.'

Hamish could have kissed her. Well…that was a given…but he *knew* she was blowing off her friends for his benefit and he seriously wanted to grab her and kiss the breath out of her. He sure as hell wanted to drag her beneath him and love her with all his strength.

All his heart.

'Oh. Right. Actually, that's a good idea,' he concurred, hoping he sounded casual and that his sister wasn't picking up on the mad echo of his heartbeat.

Grace glanced between him and Lola before cocking an eyebrow. '*You* want to go shopping instead of drinking beer?'

He shrugged. 'To be honest, I'm not sure I'm up to much company today.'

'Oh…absolutely. Of course.'

Hamish felt guilty as Grace's cynicism faded, to be replaced by an expression of concern. He didn't want her to worry about him

but he'd say whatever he needed to say to be
alone with Lola right now.

'Just don't let her drag you into a bookshop.
You'll be stuck for two hours at the travel section.'

Everyone laughed, including Lola, before
they said their goodbyes and quietly slipped
away.

'Thank you,' he murmured as they headed
for the car park. 'I really didn't want to make
polite conversation today.'

'I know.'

Hamish sucked in a breath. It was simple
but true. She did know. And he loved her for it.

Lola usually worked on Christmas Day. It was
a good excuse not to go back to Doongabi and
she got to spend it with people she really liked,
doing what she loved. Instead of with people
who wished she was different in a place that
felt just as claustrophobic as an adult as it had
when she'd been a kid.

And hospitals always went out of their way
to make everything look festive and inviting
throughout the season, and Kirribilli General
was no different.

But this Christmas morning was different.
Good different.

Waking-up-in-the-arms-of-a-sexy-man different.

Hands touching, caressing, drifting. Lips seeking, tasting, devouring. Coming together in a tangle of limbs and heavy breathing, desire and December heat slick on their skin. Crying out to each other as they came, panting heavily as they coasted through a haze of bliss and floated back down to earth.

Hitting the shower to freshen up and cool off, only to heat up again as the methodical business of soaping turned to the drugging business of pleasure. Hamish kissing her, Lola kissing him back until she couldn't breathe, couldn't stand, slumping against the tiles for support, Hamish supporting her, urging her up, her legs around him, pushing hard inside her again and groaning into her neck as he came, whispering, 'Yes, yes, yes,' as she followed him over the edge.

And that was before they got to the best bit— opening the presents.

There were only a few beneath the tree. Grace and Marcus's presents were the biggest—she'd bought them his and hers matching bathrobes as a bit of a joke present but they were top-notch quality and had cost a small fortune. They were coming over for lunch

today and Lola couldn't wait to see the looks
on their faces.

Hamish had also bought Grace a present and
it was there along with the one Lola had bought
him. It was just a novelty thing.

Nothing special. A snowglobe. With the Harbour Bridge and the Opera House planted in
the middle. It had made her smile and she figured it'd be a memento of his time here.

And maybe he'd smile too every time he
looked at it, the way he'd smiled when he'd
talked about the innkeeper's daughter in Mykonos.

The biggest surprise, though, was Hamish's
present to her, which had appeared a few days
ago. In Lola's experience, men didn't really *do*
presents for people they *loved*, let alone those
they just…slept with.

Or whatever they were doing.

What that was, Lola didn't know. But an
offer of solace had definitely turned into something more. Something she didn't want to over-
analyse. Hamish's last shift was on the second
of January and he was leaving on the third and
starting back at his Toowoomba station on the
fourth. Which meant they had just over a week
left together.

Why mess up a week of potential good hor-
izontal action—which she'd miss like crazy

when he left—to put a label on something they'd already agreed couldn't go anywhere.

'So.' Lola, who'd thrown on shorts and a red tank top with 'Dear Santa, I've been very, very bad' splashed in glittery letters across the front, was pouring them both a tall glass of orange juice in the kitchen. A Christmas CD was playing 'Frosty the Snowman' in the background. 'What say we go out to the balcony with these and open our presents?'

Hamish wrapped his arms around her from behind. He hadn't bothered with a shirt at all, just boxers, which left a lot of bare, warm skin sliding against hers. Strong thighs butted up against the backs of hers as he lowered his mouth to nuzzle her neck and Lola almost whimpered at the pleasure of it.

'I'll grab the presents,' he said.

Lola followed him out with the drinks. She sat opposite him—all the better to see him— and placed the drinks down with a tapping sound on the tabletop. The balcony was still in shade and with the Christmas music drifting out through the open doors it was a pleasant morning.

Hamish swigged half of his juice in three gulps before handing over his gift. 'Ladies first.'

Lola, who'd already had a good feel of the

present the moment he'd left the apartment, fingered it again. It was only palm-sized but quite heavy. She was dying of curiosity but also unaccountably nervous.

'No. Guests first.' She pushed his over. She'd rather break the ice with something gimmicky—have a laugh first. He started to protest but she shook her head. 'Please, Hamish, indulge me.'

He sighed dramatically but grinned and ripped the paper off. The boom of his laughter as the box was revealed had been worth it.

'Oh, my God.' He grinned as he pulled the plastic snowglobe out and shook it, holding it up between them. She watched him as his gaze followed the flakes fluttering down around the famous Sydney landmarks. 'This is awesome.'

'Yeah? You like it? I thought you'd appreciate something to take home from Sydney to remind you of the place. And the muster across the bridge.'

And her.

'Are you kidding? You know I'm nuts for all this tacky, tourist crap.' He grinned. 'It's perfect.'

Lola laughed. 'I think I win Christmas, then.'

'I think you do.' He shook it again as he held it up. 'I love it.'

His casual use of the L word caused a skip in

her pulse as her gaze narrowed to the snow falling in the dome. When she widened her gaze he was staring through the globe straight at her.

'Now you.' He placed the snowglobe on the table and tipped his chin at the present he'd given her earlier.

'Right.' She smiled as she picked it up, her fingers fumbling with the paper a little, suddenly all thumbs.

Inside the paper was a plain, thick cardboard box that had been taped by someone who obviously had shares in a sticky-tape company. Lola glanced at Hamish. 'Seriously?'

He laughed as she sighed and started on the tape. 'It's fragile. I guess they wanted to protect it as much as possible.'

Fragile? What the hell could it be?

After a minute of unravelling layers of tape, Lola was finally able to open the lid. Inside was an object secured in bubble wrap and yet more tape. She pulled that out, working away at it, going carefully as she finally revealed the most exquisite glass ornament Lola had ever seen.

It was a jacaranda tree in full flower. The gnarled trunk and its forked branches were fashioned in plain glass. The flowers, a perfect shade of iridescent blue-purple, hung from the branches, frothing in a profusion of purple, each individual bloom a teardrop of colour.

Lola blinked as she placed it reverently on the table. It was utterly breath-taking. It was delicate and feminine and so very *personal*. She didn't keep trinkets because gypsies didn't do clutter, but she knew she'd take this to the ends of the earth with her.

'I…' She glanced at him. Nobody had ever given her such an exquisite gift. 'I don't know what to say… It's utterly…*lovely*.'

'Lovely' seemed like such a bland, old-fashioned word but it was actually perfect for the piece. It was pretty and charming and sweet.

It *was* lovely.

More than that, it was *thoughtful*. Only someone who *knew* her, truly knew her would know how much something like this would mean. And the fact Hamish knew her so deeply should have her running for the hills. But all she wanted right now was to run straight into his arms.

'You like?'

'I… It's perfect.' She dragged her eyes off its loveliness to glance at him as she deliberately echoed his words. 'I love it.'

'I guess that means *I* win Christmas.'

She laughed at the tease in his voice. 'Yeah. You totally do.' She sobered as her eyes followed the graceful reach of the branches before her gaze shifted to his. 'Oh, God.' She faux-groaned. 'And I got you a crappy snowglobe that cost ten bucks.'

'Hey.' He picked up his present and held it against his naked chest as if he was trying to cover its non-existent ears. 'Don't insult the snowglobe.'

Lola laughed. There was no comparison between the two presents but he seemed just as chuffed with his gift as she was with hers.

He placed the snowglobe on the table. 'You want to see how well I can win Christmas in the bedroom?'

Lola's nostrils flared at the blatant invitation. But… 'I think you've already done that this morning. A couple of times.'

'I was just getting warmed up. Third time's the charm.'

Lola shook her head regretfully. 'I have things to prepare for lunch and a pavlova to make. Your sister's going to be here in three hours. And I think it might be a good idea if we don't look like we've spent all morning bouncing on a mattress together when she gets here.'

'I'll act my ass off, I promise. Not that I'll need to. She only has eyes for Marcus at the moment.'

Yeah. Grace was totally immersed in her new relationship, that was true. But women in love also had uncanny radar about other couples too.

'Lola Fraser, if you don't get your ass into that kitchen in the next thirty seconds, I'm going to take you remaining seated as a subconscious invitation to toss you over my shoulder, throw you on your bed and go down on you until you're singing "Ding Dong Merrily on High".'

Lola's stomach looped the loop at both the threat and the promise. 'Hold that thought,' she said as she rose and fled to the kitchen to the wicked sound of his low sexy chuckle and the jingle of bells from the CD.

CHAPTER TWELVE

THE TWO GUYS had insisted they'd clean up after Christmas lunch so Lola led Grace out onto the balcony. It was warmer outside now after several hours of the sun heating things up but there was still a nice breeze blowing in from Manly.

'Oh, my.' Grace reached for Hamish's present to Lola as she sat, turning it over and over. The sunlight caught the flowers and threw sparks of purple light across the glass of the tabletop. 'This is exquisite.'

'Yes.' Lola sipped some champagne, still stunned by the gift. 'Hamish gave it to me for Christmas.'

Lola was too caught up in the beauty of the piece to realise at first how still Grace had grown. How the light had stopped dancing on the tabletop as her hands had stopped moving. It wasn't until she spoke that Lola became aware of the situation.

'*Hamish* gave this to you?'

Lola glanced at her friend, a slight frown between her eyes at the strangled quality of Grace's voice. 'Yes.'

Grace's gaze settled on the tree for a moment before she placed it back on the table. 'I see.'

Her gaze flicked up to Lola, who frowned some more at the sudden seriousness of Grace's expression. 'What?'

'There *is* something going on between you, isn't there?'

Lola had known that Grace had been suspicious about her and Hamish a couple of times but she didn't see how a Christmas present could spark this line of questioning. Especially when she and Hamish had been impressively *chummy* throughout lunch.

'That would be stupid.' Lola trod carefully. They'd managed to keep the particulars of their relationship quiet from Grace so far. 'He's going back to Toowoomba in a week.'

'I've been watching you two for the last few hours. You've been knocking yourselves out trying to prove you're both just pals, but it's not working.'

Damn. Lola blinked, her brain searching for a rapid-fire response. She could just make out the low rumble of male voices inside over the sudden wash of her pulse through her ears and hoped like hell they stayed there until she had this sorted.

'I think you may be projecting there, Grace. Just because you're all loved up, it doesn't mean everyone else is.'

Grace sat back in her chair with a big, smug smile that was worrying and irritating all at once. 'You think I'm so caught up in my own love life that I don't notice anything else? It's been obvious today you two are sleeping together.'

Double damn. Lola swallowed, her eyes darting over Grace's shoulder to check they weren't getting any imminent visitors. She didn't need Hamish out here, making things worse. 'Obvious?'

'Sure. It's in the way you look at each other when you think the other isn't watching, all starry-eyed. And even if I was so blinded by my own feelings I couldn't see the blatantly obvious, I'd know from this.' Grace reached forward and picked up the tree again.

'It's just a Christmas present.'

'Lola.' Grace was using her don't-mess-with-me nurse voice. All nurses had one. 'This isn't *just* a Christmas gift.'

Lola glanced at the piece, a tight band squeezing her chest. 'He's…really grateful for my…hospitality these past couple of months, that's all.'

'And normally some guy you've been renting a room to would get you something for the kitchen or, better still, a gift voucher to a home appliance shop. Roomie Guy gets you practical and impersonal. He doesn't get you something pretty and frivolous. Something that's fragile and delicate and beautiful. And *meaningful.* He doesn't get you a work of art that speaks to you so deeply, that represents a place he knows you love, a place that's part of your shared history.'

Lola squirmed in her chair. She'd been so touched by the beauty of the blown glass, by its perfection, she hadn't thought about it having a deeper meaning.

Or maybe she hadn't *wanted* to.

'This is a gift of love, Lola.' Grace placed the sculpture down again. 'My brother is in love with you.'

Lola breath hitched as her gaze flew to Grace's face. *No.* How utterly ridiculous. 'He's just…a really thoughtful guy.'

She shook her head slowly. 'Trust me, I know him. He's really not. He's my brother and I love him but he's more the gimmicky gift giver.'

Lola thought about the T-shirt he'd bought Grace and his penchant for tacky snowglobes. Was Grace right? Adrenaline coursed through her system at the thought of it. She knew Hamish *liked* her. A lot. And it was reciprocated. They got on really well, enjoyed each other's company and they were magic between the sheets.

But they'd only known each other for a couple of months. It was just…fun.

Starry-eyed, Grace had called them. But really good sex *could* put stars in your eyes. It had certainly put stars in hers. And Grace's, for that matter.

'He's…going home in a week.'

'Yes.' Grace nodded, her expression gentle but earnest. 'Broken-hearted probably.'

Lola's blood surged thick and sluggish through her veins as she stared at the miniature glass sculpture. This wasn't the way it was supposed to be. They may have blurred the boundaries but he knew her attitude towards relationships and about her gypsy lifestyle. She'd thought he'd understood.

He *had* understood it, damn it. So Grace had to be wrong.

Lola was going to confront him about it as soon as Grace and Marcus had left. He'd deny it and they'd laugh over his sister's silliness and it'd be okay.

Although maybe they should *stop* sleeping together…

'More champagne, good women?'

Marcus's jovial voice coming from behind ripped Lola out of her panic. Her gaze briefly locked with Grace's, who was still eyeing her meaningfully before she turned and smiled. 'Yes, please.'

Hamish was there too, smiling at her, and the stars in his eyes blazed at her so brightly it was like a physical punch to her gut. *Crap.* She turned quickly back to escape their pull, her gaze landing squarely on Grace and her imperiously cocked *I told you so* eyebrow.

It couldn't be true. She wouldn't *let* it be true.

Hamish was standing at the sink, washing up, a couple hours later when Lola returned from seeing off their guests. 'Did they leave or did they make a pit stop in my bedroom for a quickie?' He grinned at her over his shoulder. 'I swear those two couldn't stop looking at each other.'

A faint smile touched her lips but it didn't reach her eyes. She folded her arms as she leant into the doorframe. 'That's exactly what Grace said about us.'

Hamish's smile slowly faded. Lola looked serious. In fact, she'd been kinda serious this past couple of hours. *This couldn't be good.* 'Does she know we've been sleeping together?'

'Yeah.'

'You told her?'

'No.' Lola shook her head. 'She guessed.'

'Impossible.' Hamish smiled, trying to lighten the mood. 'I acted my ass off today.'

She didn't return his smile, just dropped her gaze to the floor somewhere near his feet. 'It was your Christmas present to me.'

Hamish frowned. 'The tree?'

'She said it was a gift of love.' She raised her gaze and pierced Hamish to the spot with it, her chin jutting out. 'She said you were in love with me.'

It was softly delivered but, between the accusation in her tone and the look in her eyes, the statement hit him like a sledgehammer to the chest.

What the hell? Was Grace trying to sabotage his chances with Lola?

'Is it true?'

Of course it was true. But he hadn't wanted to tell her like this. Not that he'd given this moment much thought but he didn't want it to come when he was backed into a corner either.

Hamish dried his hands on the tea towel he had slung over his shoulder and turned round fully. 'Lola, I—'

'Is it true?' Her eyes flashed, her jaw tightened and her knuckles turned white as her fin-

gers gripped her arms hard. 'I told her it was ridiculous.'

Hamish let out a shaky breath. She was giving him an out and he could see in her eyes that she wanted him to take it. He could pick up that lie and run with it and try and salvage something out of this mess. Paper things over, spend this next week with her as if tonight hadn't happened. Then take things slowly with her over the next year—settle into something long distance.

Woo her.

But loving her was bigger than that. Bigger than him and her. Bigger than any will for it not to be so. Too big to dishonour with denial.

Too *important*.

He rested his butt against the edge of the sink. 'It's not. Ridiculous. It's true. I've fallen in love with you.'

His lungs deflated, the air rushing out with the words. He'd held them in for too long and it felt good to finally have them out. He didn't realise they'd been a weight on his chest until they weren't there any more.

Lola, on the other hand, looked as if she'd picked up those words and was being crushed beneath them, her face running the gamut from shock to disbelief to downright anger.

'But…that's not what we were doing.'

'I know.'

'I told you, I don't do relationships. We want different things.'

'I know.'

'This is just…sex, Hamish.'

'No.' He shook his head emphatically. God knew where they'd go from here but Hamish wasn't going to pretend any more that this had only been physical. And he wasn't going to let her pretend it either. It had been deeper than that right from the start.

Right from the first time she'd turned to him. Their connection had been forged that night and he knew she'd felt it too.

'It's never been just a sex thing, Lola.'

Her arms folded tighter, her lips flattened into a grim line. 'It has for me.'

A sudden rush of frustration propelled Hamish off the sink and across the kitchen, leaving only a couple of steps between them.

'Please don't lie to yourself, Lola. This is me, Hamish. I might not have known you for very long but I think you've let me in more than you've ever let anyone else in. You've told me about where you're from and your family and how you never fitted in and your Great-Aunt May and you've taken me into your bed time after time after time, even though you're the one-and-done Queen. Hell…you took me to your favourite place in Sydney. A place you've *never taken anyone else*. So don't pretend that all we've been doing is having great sex because that's ridiculous and we both know it.'

Hamish was breathing hard by the time he'd got that off his chest but he wasn't done yet either. If he was unloading everything, he should go all the way. He took the last two steps between them and slid his hands onto her arms and said, 'And I think you have feelings for me too.'

Now he was done.

She gasped, her pinched mouth forming an outraged O as she wrenched out of his grasp, pushing past him to pace the kitchen floor. 'Now *you're* being ridiculous.'

Hamish blinked at her vehement reaction. If he wasn't so sure about their connection, her dismissiveness might have cut him to the quick. 'Would it be so terrible, Lola?' His gaze followed her relentlessly back and forth as he leaned his shoulder on the doorframe. 'To let me love you? To let yourself fall in love with me?'

She stopped abruptly, her hair flying around her head as she glared at him. If anything, she was even more furious, her chest rapidly rising and falling. 'And how do you think that would work?' she demanded, her eyes wild and fiery.

'I don't know... I hadn't really thought about it.'

She gave a small snort. 'Well, think about it,' she snapped. 'Are you going to commute between here and Toowoomba or wherever the hell you end up?'

Hamish rubbed his hand along his scruffy jawline. 'I don't know.'

'Or are you going to move here?'

The rejection of that notion tingled on his tongue in a second. Sydney was a great place to visit but it'd drive him mad to live here permanently. The thought made the country boy inside him shudder. Also, he'd be putting his dream for rural service on hold. Maybe indefinitely.

But he could do it, especially if it meant being with her. 'Yes.' He nodded. 'I would move here.'

She gaped at him. 'You'd just give up all your dreams?'

'For you, yes.' He could get new dreams. What he couldn't ever get again was someone like Lola.

She was the *one*.

'If you were serious about being in a committed relationship with me,' Hamish continued, his thoughts starting to crystallise. 'Not if you're just going to keep me for a few months and discard me when your next wild adventure calls you. I'm happy to live with you wherever you want, but I'm not going to be just some filler, Lola, somebody to occupy yourself with between jaunts. I'm not going to be your *Sydney* guy.'

'God, Hamish...' She shook her head and started to pace again. 'I don't want you to give up your dreams.'

'Okay so...' Hamish shrugged. 'Come and live mine with me.'

She halted again. 'Oh, I see, so *I'm* supposed to follow you to Outer Whoop-Whoop.'

'I don't know. Maybe... Why not?' Hamish *didn't* know, but surely it was worth giving them a shot?

'Because I'm *not* going back to some speck on the map in the middle of bloody nowhere. I've paid my small-town dues, Hamish.'

'I'm not talking about forever, Lola. I'm talking about a couple of years. That's all. And it's not like it was when you were growing up in Doongabi. There's better roads and cars and more regional airports than ever being serviced by national carriers. Just because we might live in a small town, doesn't mean you're going to be *stuck* there. I'm not going to keep you a prisoner.

'You want to go to the nearest city for a week of shopping, go for it. You want to fly to Sydney to see the ballet or Melbourne to watch the tennis or the Whitsundays to lie on a beach and get a tan—great.'

She shoved her hands on her hips. 'I'm *going* to Zimbabwe in April.'

Hamish sighed. She was so damn determined to stay on the path she'd forged for herself. She been concentrating so hard on it she didn't realise she could change direction or forge a whole new path and that was okay. 'Then I'll carry your bags.'

She huffed out a breath, clearly annoyed by his logic. 'And what about my *job*?'

He shrugged. 'Rural areas are desperate for nurses.'

'But there won't be an ICU in the middle of nowhere, will there? Why should I let my skills languish?'

'Just because there won't be an ICU, doesn't mean there won't be patients who require critical care from time to time. Who are going to depend on you and what you do with what you have to keep them alive until they can be transferred to a major hospital. Think of the challenge and the experience you could come away with. I'm looking on it as a means to becoming a better paramedic, to push me, to challenge me. It could be the same for you. When was the last time you were truly challenged at work?'

An intensive care nurse had highly special-ised skills but there was a lot of support in a big city unit with not a lot of autonomy.

She folded her arms and regarded him for long moments, which was a nice change from pacing and glaring, and for a second Hamish thought he might have won her over. But finally she shook her head.

'It's not just about moving to a small town, Hamish.'

He cocked an eyebrow. 'What, then?'

'I don't want to tie myself to one person at all but if I did, it wouldn't be a small-town guy. He'd have to be a kindred spirit. He'd have to have a gypsy soul, not someone who's content to live a small life with a side of snowglobe tourism.'

Her barbs struck him dead centre. She hadn't hurled them at him but he felt the bite of them nonetheless and a spurt of anger pulsed into his system. He didn't like her insinuation that because he wasn't as well travelled as her, he was unadventurous and lacking ambition.

Being happy with his life and his lot hadn't ever been a negative in Hamish's book. He'd never considered being content a *bad* thing and the fact that she was judging him for it was extremely insulting.

He may not be worldly enough for her but he knew people didn't get to pick and choose who they had feelings for—that just happened. And ignoring it was a recipe for disaster.

Whether Lola wanted to or not, she *did* have feelings for him. Feelings he suspected scared the living daylights out of her. And not just because she had them but because he was the opposite of what she'd always told herself she wanted.

Hamish took a steadying breath, shaking off her insult. 'I think you do want someone to tie you down. That you don't want to be a gypsy all your life.'

She shook her head vehemently. 'That's the most absurd thing I've ever heard.'

Hamish probed her gaze, holding hers, refusing to let her look away. The more he talked, the more convinced he was. 'Is it? I've never pretended to be anything other than a small-town guy, Lola, and yet you went there anyway. If you didn't really want this, want me, then why have you kept coming back? What the hell has this been?'

She took a deep breath before levelling him with a serious gaze. 'A mistake.'

Hamish wouldn't have thought two little words could have had so much power. Had she yelled them at him, he could have put it down to the heat of the moment, but she was calm and deliberate, her gaze fixed on his as she shot them at him like bullets from a gun.

He couldn't speak for a beat or two. Hamish knew that whatever happened between them after today he would *never* categorise their interlude as a mistake. He would look back at it with fondness, not regret.

But right now her rejection stung.

He nodded slowly. 'Right. Okay, then.' He pushed off the doorframe. 'I think I'm going to go and stay at Grace's tonight.'

There were only so many insults a man could take in one night. Lola had called him small town and insular and now a mistake. He couldn't work out if he was angry with her or disappointed, but he couldn't stay. They would either get into it more or they'd end up in bed together because sex seemed to be the only way they dealt with emotional situations.

And he didn't have the stomach for either.

A little frown knitted her brows and she opened her mouth. For a second Hamish thought she might be going to retract everything but her mouth shut with an audible click and her chin lifted. 'That might be best.'

Hamish nodded. Her dismissal hurt but what else had he expected? 'Merry bloody Christmas, Lola.'

CHAPTER THIRTEEN

It was nine that night when Lola answered the phone. She knew who it was before she even picked up. Aunty May always rang her on Christmas morning and where she was, in the Pyrenees, it was six in the morning.

'Merry Christmas, sweetie.' Her aunt's voice crackled down the line, not as youthful as it had once been but still shot with an unflappability that was uniquely May.

Lola almost burst into tears at its familiarity. She didn't, but it was a close call as she cleared her throat and said, 'Merry Christmas, Aunty May. How's the skiing?'

May launched into her usual enthusiastic spiel she went into when she was somewhere new and Lola was grateful for the distraction. She let her aunt talk, content to throw in the odd approving noise or question, not really keeping track of the conversation, her brain far too preoccupied.

Ever since Hamish had walked out so calmly a few hours ago, Lola had been able to think of little else. It had been an incredibly crappy end to such a great day. From the second Grace had mentioned the L word it had started to go downhill and had slid rapidly south.

Damn Grace.

And damn Hamish for ruining it even further by backing up his sister's outrageous claim. They'd had another week. They could be in bed right now, enjoying their last days together. Enjoying this day in the same way it had started.

But he had to go and tell her he loved her. Tell her he knew she had feelings for him too! The fact that he was right—there was something between them, although it couldn't possibly be *love*—had only compounded the situation.

'It's been a few years since I've done a black run but I'm very much looking forward to it.'

Lola tuned back in. 'It's just like riding a bike.' Aunt May had been skiing for the better part of fifty years—she could out-ski Lola any day.

May burst out with one of her big, hooting laughs. 'Been a while since I rode one of those too. Never mind... I've made some friends with a couple of hottie old widowers here so I won't be alone.'

And she launched into an entertaining description of the two gents in question in that irreverent way of hers that always kept Lola in stitches. Except for tonight. Because all Lola could think about was Hamish and how abominable she'd been to him.

Yes, he'd admitted he loved her and that had been a shock, but he hadn't deserved being told he was living a small life and that he was a mistake. As someone who'd made her fair share of mistakes she could confidently say none of them had felt as good as Hamish.

She'd even opened her mouth to apologise, to take it back, but then she'd realised it had been the perfect shield to fight the sword of his L word and she'd left it. But she hadn't liked herself very much.

And she liked herself even less now.

'Okay, sweetie. Are you going to tell me what's on your mind?'

Lola blinked. Aunty May was ten thousand kilometres away and they were speaking down a phone line but she still knew something was up. 'What? Nothing.' She forced herself to laugh. 'I'm fine. Just a little tired, that's all.'

'Lola Gwendolyn Fraser. This is me. When will you learn you can't fool your old Aunty May?'

Lola gripped the phone. It was some kind of

irony that a woman who had been largely absent from her life knew her so well. They had that kindred spirit connection.

'Does it have anything to do with that guy who's been staying with you? What's his name again?'

'Hamish.' Even saying his name made Lola feel simultaneously giddy and depressed.

'That's right. Grace's brother.'

'Yes.'

'And you're in love with him?'

'No!' Tears blurred Lola's vision. 'I've only known him for two months.'

There was silence for a moment. 'You showed him your jacarandas, right?'

Lola was beginning to wish she'd never told May or Grace that particular bit of information. 'Yes, but I'm like you. A gypsy. We travel. We don't fall in love.'

'Poppycock!'

Lola blinked at the rapid-fire dismissal.

'It took me two minutes to fall in love with Donny.'

Donny? Who the hell was Donny? And since when had her spinster aunt been in love with anyone? 'Donny?'

'The one great love of my life.'

What the—? 'I...didn't know there'd been anyone.'

It was a weird concept to wrap her head around—her spinster aunt in love with a man. Lola had no doubt she'd been highly sought after but May had always been staunchly single.

'Well…it was a long time ago now.'

The wistfulness in her great-aunt's voice squeezed fingers around Lola's already bruised heart. 'What happened?'

May said nothing for a beat or two as if she was trying to figure out where to start. 'I was seventeen, working at the haberdashery in Doongabi, and this dashing young police officer moved to town. He was thirty. But when you know, you *know*.' She gave a soft chuckle. 'I fell hopelessly in love.'

'I see.' That was quite an age gap even for fifty-something years ago. 'And that caused a stir in the family? Or…' She hesitated. 'Didn't he reciprocate?'

Lola thought it the least likely option. May had always been a tall, handsome woman. Carried herself well, wore clothes well. But in the photos Lola had seen of her as a teenager she'd been striking, with an impish flicker in her eyes.

'Oh, he reciprocated. It was wonderful.' She sighed and there was another pause. 'But he was married. He had a wife and two girls who were joining him a little later. And I knew it and I embarked on a liaison with him anyway.'

Married? 'Oh.' Lola hadn't expected that.

'Yes. Oh... So I left. The day before his family were due in town. I was afraid if I stayed I wouldn't give him up, I wouldn't end it. That I'd risk my family's reputation and his marriage and break up his home because I was young and selfish and loved him too much.'

A lump lodged in Lola's throat. May was rattling it off as if it was something that had happened to somebody else but she couldn't hide the thickness in her voice—not from Lola.

'I'm so sorry. I didn't know.'

'It's fine.' May cleared her voice. 'As I said, it was in a whole other lifetime.'

'Is he still—?'

'No.' Her aunt cut her off. 'He died ten years ago. But you know...' She gave a half laugh, half sigh that echoed with young love. 'I would give up everything I've ever done, every place I've ever been, to have spent my life with him.'

Lola sat forward in the chair. *'What?'*

'Oh, yes. I've been with other men, Lola. Even loved a few of them. But not like Donny. He was always the one.'

'But...you've had such a wonderful life.'

'Yes, I have. I've been very lucky.'

'Right.' Lola nodded, feeling suddenly like

she was the elder in the conversation having to point out the obvious. 'You've been to so many places. Seen so many things. Your life has been so full.'

'No, sweetie, it hasn't. I've been living a half-life. There's always been something missing. So promise me not to make the same mistake I did, choosing adventure over love. If this man loves you and if you love him, as I suspect you just might, be open to it. Humans are meant to love and be loved. We mate for life. And a gypsy caravan is big enough for two.'

Lola was too stunned to speak. Her whole world had just shifted on its axis. Not only had her great-aunt had a torrid affair with an older, married man but she'd have traded her gypsy life for a second chance with him.

'Lola? Promise me.'

Her aunt's voice was fierce and strong and Lola was spooked by the sudden urgency of it, goose-bumps breaking out on her arms. 'I promise.'

Lola was pleased to be back at work the next morning. Between what had happened with Hamish and the conversation with her great-aunt, her head was spinning. May—spinster of seventy-five years—had loved a married man she'd gladly have given everything up for. And Hamish *loved* her.

Loved.

On such short acquaintance. And having being warned that she didn't *do* love.

The whole world had gone mad.

At least work was sane. She knew what she was doing there. What was expected of her. And people didn't ask more than they knew she could give. She could care there, she could give a piece of herself, but she didn't have to give them *everything*. They didn't demand her heart and soul.

Only her mind and body. And *that* she could do.

'Lola, can you take Emma today, please? She's due to be transferred to the ward around eleven so can you make sure all her discharge stuff is completed by morning tea?'

'Yep. Sure can.' Lola leapt up from her chair in the staffroom, eager to throw her body and mind into a full, busy shift. And she was excited to be the nurse looking after Emma on her last day on the unit.

Everything since the transplant had gone swimmingly well and Lola was thrilled about Emma's transfer. Two months was a long time to be on the ICU and all the nurses had grown fond of Emma and her lovely supportive family.

For so long it had been touch and go and to see her leaving the unit with a new heart and a new chance at life was why Lola did what she did.

'Hey,' Lola said as she approached Emma's bed to take handover from the night nurse. The background noise of beeping monitors and trilling alarms and tubes being suctioned formed a comforting white noise that blocked out the yammering in her brain.

'Hey, Lola.'

Emma's voice was still husky but she beamed at Lola. She'd lost weight, was as weak as a kitten and looked like she'd been in a boxing ring with her smattering of scars, nicks and old bruises, but the sparkle in her eyes told Lola everything she needed to know. Emma's spirit was strong, she was a fighter. And she was going to be okay.

'I'll just get handover and then we'll get you all ready for your discharge to the ward.'

'Now, those are some beautiful words,' Emma quipped. The small white plaster covering her almost healed tracheostomy incision crinkled with her neck movement.

Lola took handover. It was short and quick compared to the previous weeks that had required twenty minutes to chronicle all the drugs and infusions and changes as well as the ups and downs of the shift.

'How did you sleep?' Lola asked a few minutes later as she performed her usual checks of all the emergency equipment around the bed.

Emma may be leaving in a few short hours but certain procedures were ingrained for Lola. It was important to know everything she might need in an emergency was here, exactly where it was located and that it was in full working order.

Patient safety always came first.

'Wonderfully.'

Lola laughed. 'Somebody should have warned me I was going to need sunglasses today to block out the brightness of your smile.'

'I am pretty excited about leaving this dump,' Emma said with a smile.

Lola sighed and clutched her chest dramatically. 'People never want to stay.'

Emma grinned. 'I'll come back and visit.'

Lola grinned too as she put a stethoscope in her ears. 'Make sure you do.' She placed the bell on Emma's chest and listed to her breathing. A patient assessment was performed at the start of every shift.

'You want to know what I got for Christmas?' Emma asked as Lola removed the earpieces. 'Besides a new heart?'

Lola cocked an eyebrow—Emma was vibrating with excitement. 'Of course.' Hopefully it'd help take her mind off what Hamish had got her. The little glass jacaranda tree had caused a shedload of problems.

Emma held up her left hand and wiggled her fingers. The oxygen saturation trace on the monitor went a little haywire because the probe was on that hand but that wasn't what caught Lola's attention. A big, fat diamond ring sparkled in the sunshine slanting in through the open vertical blinds covering the windows.

'Barry asked me to marry him and I said yes.'

Lola blinked as the refraction shone in her eyes. Damn it, was the whole world conspiring against her at the moment?

'Crikey.' Lola kept her voice light and teasing as she took Emma's hand and inspected it closely, her heart beating a little harder at the expression of pure joy on her patient's face. 'Did he rob that bank he works for?' Barry was a teller at a bank in the city.

Emma laughed. 'I'm afraid to ask.'

Lola smiled as she released Emma's hand. 'Well, I'm thrilled for you. If anyone deserves a bit of happiness it's you.'

Emma held her hand out to admire the ring, wriggling her fingers slightly to get a real sparkle going. 'To think I was never going to do this. Marriage and all that stuff.'

Lola had turned to grab a pair of gloves from the windowsill behind so she could remove the arterial line from Emma's wrist, but she stopped and turned back. 'Oh?'

Maybe this was why she felt such an affinity for Emma? She too didn't want to tie herself down.

'Yeah.' Emma dropped her hand to her stomach. 'Baz and I have only been going out for ten months and he's asked me twice to marry him now but I always felt like I was a bad bet for a guy. Why would I inflict a woman with a dodgy ticker on someone I supposedly loved without an easy out for him? Better for him to just be able to walk away, for us both to be able to when things got tough.'

'I see.'

'Barry's kinda hard to shake, though.' Emma grinned. 'He was determined to stick around. To show me that he was here for the long haul as well as the short haul if that's the way it panned out.'

Lola nodded. 'He's been very dedicated, Emma. He was here every day.'

'Yeah, I know. But even with my new heart… well…' Emma grimaced. 'The potential for complications is real, right? Rejection, infection, complications from medication…and how long will it last till I need another one? But when he asked me yesterday morning to marry him, all that just fell away and love was all that mattered.'

A lump the size of Emma's bed lodged in Lola's throat. Isn't that what May had essentially said last night too? If Lola didn't know better, she'd say the universe was trying to tell her something.

Just as well she didn't go in for all that spiritual crap.

'Sure, my life's potentially shorter than that of other women my age and it might not all be smooth sailing, but none of us are guaranteed a long life, are we? I mean, I don't know how old my donor was but he or she didn't get a say in their life coming abruptly to an end, right?'

Lola nodded. It was still a miracle to her that they'd managed to pull off having a donor and a recipient on the same unit without either being aware of the other.

'Life's short, I know that better than anyone, so why shouldn't I get to live my life fully? Like other people? To love like other people. To share my life, no matter how long it is, with someone else? And I think I owe that to my donor. To live my life *fully*. Why should I restrict myself to a half-life?'

A half-life. Just as May had said last night.

'Of course you do,' Lola said, a little spooked that Emma appeared to be channelling her great-aunt. 'You deserve all the good things, Emma, and I think it's exactly what your donor would have wanted.'

Emma smiled and grabbed her hand. 'So do you, Lola.' For a second Lola's heart stopped—maybe her patient actually *was* channelling Aunty May—but then Emma glanced around the unit at the general hubbub. 'All the nurses do. You're freaking angels.'

Lola gave her usual self-deprecating smile. 'Okay, well, there's no time to shine my halo at the moment.' She squeezed Emma's hand before withdrawing it, all business now. 'I've gotta spring you out of here.'

Emma nodded and sighed and went back to looking at her engagement ring.

CHAPTER FOURTEEN

THERE WAS A knock on Lola's door later that afternoon. She'd just shoved the ice cream in the freezer and ripped into a chocolate bar. She might as well have one of those too if she was about to consume a one-litre tub of ice cream, right?

The knock came again and she put the bar down with an impatient little noise at the back of her throat. 'Coming.'

Her pulse accelerated as she walked towards the door—what if it was Hamish? She had no idea what his plans were for his last week. Was he coming back? His stuff was still all here, or was he going to move in with Grace for his remaining time?

She felt sure if it was him he'd probably just use his key but maybe, after their words yesterday, he didn't want to intrude uninvited. Her heart did a funny little giddy-up at the thought.

It'd only been twenty-four hours but she missed his face.

It wasn't Hamish.

It was the police. Two of them—a man and a woman, both in neat blue uniforms and wearing kindly expressions.

Lola frowned. 'Can I help you?'

The woman introduced them. 'Are you Miss Fraser?'

'Yes, that's right...' Although she felt rather stupid being called 'miss' at the age of thirty. 'Lola.'

'You are the next of kin for a May Fraser?' she clarified.

The hair on Lola's nape prickled. 'Yes. She's my aunt. My great-aunt.' Lola had been down as May's emergency contact for the last ten years. 'Is something wrong?'

Had her aunt fallen on that black run and broken something? Her leg? Or a hip? She was going to be really cranky with herself if she had. But then something worse occurred to her. The police didn't usually come around just to tell someone their loved one had been injured in a foreign land.

But...what if it was more serious than that? What if there'd been an avalanche? A surge of adrenaline flew into Lola's system.

'Could we come in?'

The question was alarming. 'Please just tell me here.' Because if they could tell her here, *whatever it was*, on the doorstep, then it couldn't be too bad, right?

Lola didn't notice the barely perceptible exchange of glances that passed between the two police officers. 'I think it would be better if we came in, Lola,' the male officer said gently, his smile kind.

Oh, God. Dread burrowed into her veins and the lining of her gut and the base of her skull but Lola fell back automatically to admit them. Once they were sitting, the male officer took up the baton and delivered the news she'd been expecting.

'I'm sorry to have to inform you, Lola, but your Aunt May passed away earlier today.'

Every cell and muscle in Lola's body snap froze. Aunty May was…*dead*? The pounding of her heartbeat rose in her ears as tears sprang to her eyes, scalding and instant.

May was dead.

'Did she…have a skiing accident?' Lola wasn't sure if it was the right thing to ask but her mind was a blank and it seemed logical given what she knew about May's whereabouts and her intended activity.

'No.' The woman took over now as if they were some kind of grief tag team and for a second Lola thought how horrible it must be to deliver this kind of news as part of your *job*.

Lola had sat through many end-of-life conversations in hospitals, holding the hands of distressed and grieving people. But this? Out of the blue like this? Everything chugging along then *bam!* Strangers on your doorstep.

'She was found in her bed,' the woman continued. 'She didn't turn up to meet some people she was going to go skiing with and they raised the alarm. Hostel staff entered her room to find her still in her bed. At first they thought she was sleeping but they couldn't rouse her. She'd died some time during the night in her sleep.'

Lola shook her head. Died in her sleep. *No.* Whenever she'd imagined her aunt's death it'd been her doing something adventurous when she was ninety-seven.

Going out with a bang, not a whimper.

'But… I was just talking to her yesterday.' Which was a stupid thing to say given her medical background—she knew how quickly and unexpectedly death could come knocking. 'She was fine. Are you sure?'

May's words from the phone call came back to her now and Lola shivered. They'd spooked her a little yesterday but even more so now. May's insistence that Lola promise her to give love a chance felt like some kind of portent today.

Was that only twenty-four hours ago?

Had her great-aunt *known* she was not long for this world?

Goose-bumps feathered Lola's arms at the thought.

'Yes. I'm afraid so.' The man again with his gentle voice. 'It's been confirmed by all the appropriate officials.'

'Could it have been…some kind of foul play?'

It seemed like a bizarre thing to ask but no more bizarre than her bulletproof aunt dying in her sleep.

The police officers took her question in their stride. 'The local authorities say that your aunt was lying peacefully in her bed wearing her sleep mask.'

Lola almost laughed at that piece of information. May used to collect the sleep masks from airlines and swore by them as an antidote to jet-lag. She'd never travelled without one.

'There'll be an autopsy, of course, but they're expecting to find natural causes.'

Lola nodded, the medical side of her brain already making guesses. It had probably been a massive stroke or a heart attack. It wouldn't have been a bad way to go, a quick death, taking her in the night. But the thought May had died alone was like a knife to Lola's chest.

It would have been the way her aunt would have wanted it—dying as she'd lived—but Lola wished she'd been able to hug her one last time and she thanked the universe for that phone call yesterday. She was grateful for the time they'd spent chatting, for having spoken to her beloved aunt one last time.

Even if May's words hadn't sat easily on Lola's shoulders.

The officers talked more about procedures and passed over some pamphlets regarding relatives who died overseas. 'Is there someone we can call for you, Lola? Someone who can be with you now?'

Hamish.

His was the first name that popped into Lola's head and a tidal wave of emotion swamped her chest. Her fingers curled in her lap as she thought about the solid comfort of his arms around her, about him holding her, keeping her together while her insides leaked out.

But she couldn't. Not after their argument. Grace came to mind next but as she had lied to her best friend about sleeping with her brother *and* ignored six phone calls from her in the last twenty-four hours, she didn't feel able to suggest that either.

Of course, Grace wouldn't care about any of that in the face of this news. But Lola wasn't exactly thinking straight at the moment.

'Um, no.' She shook her head. 'I'm good. I'm fine.' Her mouth stretched into a smile that felt like it had been drawn on her face in crayon.

'We don't like leaving people alone after this kind of news,' the male officer said. 'Especially at Christmas.'

Between the events of yesterday and working today, Lola had forgotten it was Christmas. 'It's okay. Really. I'm a nurse, I work at the Kirribilli in ICU. I'll be fine.'

That information seemed to relax them both.

'I'll ring my mum,' Lola assured them. 'May is *her* aunt. And we'll go from there.' She smiled more genuinely this time, realising that her last attempt had probably frightened the hell out of them. 'I'll be fine, I promise.'

They left with her assurances but the last thing Lola felt like right now was talking to her mother. She *would* ring her—in a while. Right now she felt too numb to use her fingers, to use words. She needed time to wrap her head around the fact she was never going to see her favourite person in the whole world ever again.

Lola sat on the couch and fell sideways, pulling her legs up to her chest. Tears pricked at her eyes. May was gone. No more Christmas Day phone calls. No more postcards. No more random drop-ins. No more *National Geographic*-like pictures or entertaining foreign swear words or endlessly fascinating anecdotes from her travels.

May hadn't just been some distant, eccentric great-aunt. She'd been Lola's family. She'd been the one who had understood her when no one else had. She'd been Lola's sounding board, her shoulder to cry on when life in Doongabi had seemed like it would never come to an end, and had championed her desire to travel and see the world.

Lola realised suddenly she was already thinking of May in the past tense and pain, like a lightning bolt, stabbed her through the heart with its jagged heat, stealing her breath. The first tear rolled down her cheek. Then the next and the next until there was a puddle.

And the puddle became a flood.

Hamish stood indecisively outside Lola's door much the same as he had almost two months ago now. Nervous and unsure of himself. He'd been furious when he'd walked out yesterday and while he'd calmed down significantly, he was still a little on the tense side. He couldn't remember ever knowing a woman he wanted to shake as badly as he wanted to drag her clothes off and kiss her into submission.

He got it, she was used to keeping her relationships in a box, one where she made all the rules and had all the control.

But to not be open to something more? Something different? Something deeper?

Something *better*?

It was ironic that Lola had left Doongabi partly because everyone she'd known had been stuck in their ways and yet she was proving to be just as immovable.

He knocked, wary of his reception. Not knowing if she was even home. He knew she'd worked an early shift today, which meant she'd normally be home by now, but maybe she'd made other plans.

And what was he going to say if she *was* home? What was his plan? Hamish knew what he wanted. He wanted to come back here for his last remaining days. Back into Lola's house and her bed and her *life* and make plans with her. Plans about how their future might work out. It wouldn't be easy to come up with something they were both happy with but he knew they could do it if they put their minds to it.

If they both committed.

But if Lola didn't want any part of a future with him? Could he live here for the next week and pretend he was okay with her decision? Pretend he wasn't dying a little each day?

Whatever…they needed to have a conversation which was why he'd come now and not earlier when he'd known she'd be at work. They'd both had twenty-four hours to mull over what had gone down yesterday and he could sit and brood and look obsessively at the picture he'd taken of her that day with jacaranda flowers in her hair, or he could confront her.

He'd chosen confrontation. It was time to lay their cards on the table.

Hamish knocked again. When she still didn't answer he sighed and fished in his pocket for his keys. He'd have preferred to enter by invitation but if she wasn't home it wasn't going to happen. And, if nothing else, he needed his clothes for work tomorrow.

He inserted the key into the lock. He'd just grab his bag and go. Ring her later and see if they could make a time to talk. He entered the apartment and pulled the door shut behind him, the ghosts of a hundred memories trailing him as he traversed the short entrance alcove that opened into the living room.

'Hamish?'

Her head and torso suddenly popped up from the couch and scared the living daylights out of him. Hamish clutched his chest to still his skyrocketing pulse. 'Damn it, Lola.'

'Sorry.'

'I knocked but…'

It was then he noticed her red-rimmed eyes and her blotchy face in stark relief to the pallor of her skin. She looked…awful. Lost and scared and small. Like someone had knocked the stuffing out of her. Not the strong, feisty Lola he was used to.

Was this grief…over him? Over them?

And why was the thought as gratifying as it was horrifying? What the hell was wrong with him?

'Lola?' Hamish took a step towards her but stopped, unsure of how welcoming she'd be to his offer of solace. 'Are you okay?'

Her short hysterical-sounding laugh did not allay his concerns. She shook her head, her curls barely shifting it was so slight. 'Aunty May died.'

Her words dropped like stones into the fraught space between them. 'What?' *Her aunt was dead?*

He was at her side in three strides, their animosity forgotten as he sank down beside her, his hand sliding around her shoulder and pulling her to him. She didn't argue or jerk away, just whimpered like a wounded animal and melted into his side.

He eased them back against the couch and her arm came around his stomach, her head falling to his shoulder. Hamish dropped his chin to her springy curls, shutting his eyes as he caught a whiff of his coconut shampoo in her hair.

'You want to talk about it?'

She shook her head. 'Not yet.'

So he just held her. Held her while her tears flowed, silently at first then louder, choking on her sobs, her shoulders shaking with the effort to restrain herself and failing. Eventually her sobs settled to hiccupping sighs and she was able to talk, to tell him what had happened.

'I'm so sorry,' Hamish murmured, still cradling her against him, his lips in her hair. He knew how much Lola's great-aunt meant to her.

Lola nodded. 'I thought she'd be around for ever, you know?'

'Yeah.' He dropped another kiss on her head. 'I know.'

She seemed to collect herself then, pushing away from him slightly as she scrubbed at her face with her hands. 'Sorry for crying all over you.'

'Don't.' Hamish cupped her cheek, wiping at

some moisture she'd missed. 'I want to be here for you, Lola. You *have* to know that.'

He wanted to be here for her for ever. If she'd let him.

Emotion lurked in her big green eyes, waiting for another surge of grief. They slayed him, so big and bright with unshed tears.

So…damn sad.

'Hamish.' Her hand slid on top of his as their gazes locked. She absently rubbed her cheek into his palm and tiny charges of electricity travelled down his arm to his heart. From there it was a direct line to his groin.

Which made him feel like seven different kinds of deviant.

Traitorous body! *This wasn't about that.* This was about something deeper and more profound.

Comfort. Not sex.

Yet the two seemed to have a habit of intertwining where they were concerned. Even now he could feel the threads reaching out between them, twisting together, drawing them nearer.

Her breathing roughened and Hamish responded in kind. A strange kind of tension settled over them, as if the world was holding its breath. Her eyes went from moisture bright to a rich, wanton glitter.

'Lola.'

It was a warning as much for himself as for her. They couldn't keep doing this, letting desire do their talking. She was grieving. And he wanted to give her more than a quick roll on the couch. They *mustn't* let their hormones take over.

'I missed you last night,' she said, her voice barely louder than a whisper.

Apart from *I love you* she couldn't have chosen better words to say to him, especially when they were full of ache and want and need. Her voice was husky and it crawled right inside his pants and stroked.

'*Lola.*'

He was only a man. And he loved her.

She shifted then, moved closer, pressing all her curves back into him again as her mouth closed the gap between them. Their lips met and he was lost.

Gone. Swept away.

In her taste and her smell and the small little sounds of her satisfaction that filled his head and rushed through his veins like a shot of caffeine.

Hamish's other hand curved around her face, sank into her hair as he kissed her back, his nose filling with the smell of her, his tongue tingling with the taste of her. She moaned and he half turned and their bodies aligned and he totally lost his mind.

He'd missed her too.

It was a crazy thing to admit. It had only been twenty-four hours but he hadn't been able to stop thinking about her, to stop wanting her, to stop wishing he'd just shut the hell up and not pushed for more.

It wasn't fair that one woman had so much power but that was love, right? You laid yourself bare to one person. Laid yourself bare to their favour as well as their rejection.

'God... Hamish...'

Her voice was thick with need as she slid her leg over the top of his and straddled him. She kissed along his neck and pulled at his shirt and he was drowning. Happily. Being sucked down into the depths of Lola's passion, dying in her arms, every part of him aching to give her what she wanted. What she needed.

And to hell with what he wanted, what he needed.

But somewhere, something was fighting back. A single brain cell screaming at him to *stop, stop, stop.* To have some respect. For himself. And for Lola.

Groaning, Hamish wrenched his mouth away from her kiss, from her pull. 'Wait.' He shut his eyes and panted into her neck as her hands fell to his fly, her fingers not waiting one little bit. And he wanted her hand on him so damn bad.

'Stop.'

He shifted, grasping for sanity, for clarity as he tipped her off his lap. Ignoring the almost animalistic moan from Lola, he pushed to his feet and strode to the opposite side of the room. Shoving his hand high up on the wall for support, Hamish battled to control the crazy rattle of his heart and the crazier rush of his libido.

'I can't.'

She made a noise that sounded like another sob and Hamish whipped around. He couldn't do this if she started crying again.

She wasn't. But she *was* annoyed.

'I'm sorry.' It seemed like the least he could say given the frustration bubbling in her gaze and how hard her chest rose and fell.

She rubbed a hand over her face as she exhaled in a noisy rush. 'Hell, Hamish. I just… needed some comfort.'

'Yeah.' An ironic laugh rose in his throat but he choked it back. 'That's what we do, you and I, when we're feeling emotional. We have sex. That's the problem.'

'Why is it a problem?'

Her casual dismissal was like the slow drip of poison in his veins, eating away at him. 'Because we don't talk, Lola. We just take our clothes off and let our bodies do the talking. And I need more than that now. We need to start using our mouths to communicate, not our bodies.'

She blinked at him like she couldn't believe what was coming out of his mouth. But he meant every word.

'I love you. I want to *be* with you. I want to be in your life—*part of your life*—not just the person you turn to when you need some distraction between the sheets.'

Hamish broke off, his heartbeat flying in his chest. Was he making any sense? It all seemed totally jumbled inside his head.

'You want me to help you with the funeral arrangements and repatriation of May and being there when you talk to your family and rocking you as you cry yourself to sleep tonight? I can do that. I *want* to do that. I want you to lean on me, Lola. I want it all.'

She looked at him helplessly and Hamish felt lower than a snake's belly. Denying her didn't give him any satisfaction. But it would be too easy to slip into their old routine. Find himself in the kind of relationship he *didn't* want, and he couldn't bear the thought. His insides shrivelled at the prospect.

He wanted to be all in. And if that wasn't on the table then he needed to be all out.

'I…can't deal with this now, Hamish.' She rose from the couch and paced to the open balcony door. The last rays of afternoon sunlight slanted inside, gilding her shape. 'Can you please just go?'

Hamish nodded. He'd dumped a lot on her today, on top of the news about May. Which was an awful thing to do but, damn it, she drove him crazy. He wanted to be her *person*, not just a warm body with the right anatomical parts.

He sighed. 'I'll just grab my stuff and go. I'll be at Grace's until my plane leaves on the third.'

She nodded, her back erect. 'Okay.'

Hamish waited but she didn't turn around no matter how hard he willed it. 'I'll ring you tomorrow to check on you.'

She nodded again but didn't say anything, a stiff, forlorn figure in the fading gold of the afternoon light. It was like a knife to his heart to walk away. But a wise man knew when to choose his battles and live to fight another day and he was going to fight for Lola.

Even if it meant playing the long game.

CHAPTER FIFTEEN

THE APARTMENT WAS silent as Lola let herself in at almost ten thirty on New Year's Eve. Her shift had finished at nine but with the road closures around Kirribilli because of the New Year celebrations, she'd had to take public transport to work. Which had been fine on the way to the hospital but on the return journey the buses had been loaded with families trying to get home after the early fireworks. Add to that the detours in place and the trip had been much longer than usual.

Throwing her bag and a bundle of mail on the coffee table, Lola used the remote to flick on the television. Every channel was showing New Year revelry in Sydney, from shots of the foreshores to the concert on the steps of the Opera House. She settled on one channel and headed for the kitchen.

Grabbing the fridge door, Lola paused as her gaze fell on May's postcard. Her heart squeezed as she pulled it off and read it again, smiling at May's inimitable style. It still punched her in the gut to think she was never going to get another postcard from her aunt to brighten her day and make her smile every time she saw it.

The last few days had been a flurry of activity, making the arrangements to repatriate her aunt's body and coping with all the associated paperwork and legal requirements. Which had been a good thing. Something to keep Lola's mind off Hamish and how much she missed having him around.

May's body was expected back in Sydney in four days and Lola was travelling with her to Doongabi. May hadn't made any specific funeral requests, just that she be cremated and that Lola scatter her ashes somewhere wild and exotic.

Lola didn't think May would mind going home after all this time, especially knowing that her aunt had left out of propriety, not animosity. It wouldn't be her final resting place, Lola would make sure of that, but funerals weren't for the dead. They were for the living. And the town and the Fraser family wanted to be able to grieve her passing, even if it had been over fifty years since May had left.

Including Lola's mother, who had been surprisingly helpful with all the arrangements and genuinely upset at May's passing. Lola had always thought her mother had disliked her aunt for her gypsy ways and for seducing Lola to join the dark side, but her mother's grief had been raw and humbling and had made Lola look at her mother in a different light.

She put the postcard back on the fridge with a sigh, knowing without a shadow of a doubt that May's last written communication would stay right where it was for ever. Opening the door, Lola grabbed the half-empty bottle of wine and poured herself a glass. She was going to sit on the balcony in the dark and watch the revellers whooping it up at the park across the road.

She was going to think about everything that had happened this past year. About May and her mother and going back to Doongabi. About the explosion at the night club and Wesley and Emma.

And Hamish.

From their first meeting on the bridge to him walking out of here the other day, rebuffing her need for comfort. She was going to *wallow* in all of it. Probably even cry over it a little.

But when the clock struck twelve, that was it. A new year. A clean slate. Looking forward. Not back. And there was a lot to look forward to. Seeing family again. A job that she loved.

Her trip to Zimbabwe. And maybe it was time to take a sabbatical and do some more extensive travelling. Her aunt was gone, someone had to pick up her mantle.

Someone had to take May's place.

Work would probably let her take a year off without pay. And even if they refused, she could quit. It wasn't like she couldn't get another job again on her return to Australia. She was highly skilled. She could go anywhere with a hospital and pick up a job.

From Sydney to some two-bit town way out past the black stump. Which brought her squarely back to Hamish.

And just how lonely she felt suddenly, her life stretching out in front of her, a series of intersecting roads and her walking down the middle. All by herself.

Lola had never felt lonely before. Serial travellers made friends wherever they went but were also happy with their own company. When had she stopped being happy with her own company?

Maybe it was to do with her aunt's death? Knowing she was out there somewhere in Lola's corner had counteracted any isolation Lola might have felt without May in her life. But deep down she knew it was Hamish—she'd only started feeling lonely since he'd come on the scene.

Damn the man.

To distract herself, Lola contemplated going out. Throwing on her red dress and getting herself dolled up and hitting Billi's. She could probably still make it before the countdown. Flirt with some men, do some midnight kissing.

But the thought was depressing as all giddy-up. The truth was, she didn't want to be with just anyone tonight, kiss just anyone. She wanted Hamish.

Lola scowled and stood up. *It would pass.*

It was just a break up-thing, the loss of the familiar. Which was why she didn't do relationships. No relationships, no break-ups. No feeling like death warmed up on New Year's Eve or any other night for that matter.

They were too different, she reminded herself. They wanted different things. It would never work.

She went and poured herself another glass of wine, picking up the mail off the coffee table as she passed. But she didn't open it straight away, distracting herself instead with her phone and friends' social media posts.

All round the world, it seemed, people were in varying stages of preparation for the New

Year. Lots of overseas friends stared back at her from photos full of happy, smiling people, all having a great time together. She tried to smile too, to feel their joy, but she felt nothing except the heavy weight sitting on her chest.

It was grief, Lola understood that, but knowing that didn't make it any easier.

She should have volunteered to work the night shift tonight instead of the late shift she'd filled in for as at least it would have kept her mind on other things. Like how she and Hamish had requested this night off so they could sit on the foreshore together and watch the fireworks, show the country boy some real city magic.

The thought made her smile, which made her annoyed, and Lola grabbed for the mail. Maybe a few bills might help keep her mind off things until the fireworks went off and her slate was magically cleaned. She hadn't checked the box since before Christmas so she had quite a stack to deal with.

Most of it was bumf from advertisers. There were three bills, though—it was the season for credit cards after all—and a letter from the local elected representative wishing his constituents all the best for the festive season.

And there was a postcard. From May.

Lola's heart almost stopped for a moment before it sped up, racing crazily as tears scalded the backs of her eyes. It was of a snow-covered mountain, the peak swirled with clouds. The caption on the front read, 'Beauty should be shared.'

On the flipside, May had written, 'One of nature's mighty erections.' Then she'd drawn a little smiley face with a tongue hanging out. Lola burst out laughing and then she started to cry, the words blurring. Her aunt had signed off with, 'Merry Christmas, Love, May.'

'Oh, May,' Lola whispered, turning the card over again to look at the picture, her heart heavy in her chest and breaking in two. 'I'm going to miss you.'

The mountain stared back at her, and so did the words. *'Beauty should be shared.'* May's strange insistence from their Christmas Day phone call that Lola choose love over adventure, replayed in her head. *'A gypsy caravan is big enough for two.'*

Lola's heart skipped a beat as the words from the postcard took on a deeper meaning. *Beauty should be shared.* Was her aunt reaching out from beyond the grave? The feeling that May had somehow known she wasn't long for this world returned.

Suddenly Emma's words joined the procession in Lola's head.

'Why shouldn't I get to live my life fully? Like other people? To love like other people. To share my life, no matter how long it is, with someone else. Why should I restrict myself to a half-life?'

Lola shut her eyes as the words slugged hot and hard like New Year's Eve fireworks into her chest. Oh, God. That was what she was doing. She was restricting herself to a half-life. Choosing adventure over love.

Yes, love.

Because she *did* love Hamish Gibson. No matter how much she'd tried to deny it. How much it scared her. And it did scare her because they were so different and she knew squat about being a couple. Squat about being grounded after being a gypsy most of her adult life.

But he'd crept up on her, slid under all her defences, and her heart was full of him. Bursting with him. And now she couldn't imagine her life without him.

She didn't know what shape her life would take next, all she knew was that two wise women had given her advice this festive season and she'd be a fool to discard the lessons they'd imparted.

She chose love. She chose a full life.

If she hadn't already blown it.

Lola stood. Not stopping to think about what she was doing next, she was already on her phone, ordering a cab, which would probably cost her a fortune in a surcharge on New Year's Eve but she'd had two glasses of wine and she didn't care. She grabbed the postcard off the table and strode into the living room, snatching her keys out of her handbag before heading for the door.

She *had* to see Hamish. She had to tell him she loved him and beg him to forgive her and hope like hell she *hadn't* blown it. Because now Lola realised she was living a half-life and she wanted her full life, *with Hamish*, to start immediately.

Lola arrived at Grace's apartment with fifteen minutes to spare before midnight. She knew Marcus and Grace had gone to some fancy party in the city so they wouldn't be here. She also knew Hamish wasn't working.

Because they were supposed to be together tonight.

She just hoped like hell he was at the apartment and not out somewhere whooping it up, because he wasn't answering her calls or her texts. If he wasn't here she didn't know what she was going to do, but if it meant she had to sleep outside this door all night, torturing herself with images of who he might be whooping it up with, she would.

Lifting her hand to knock, the door opened before she got a chance to make contact and Lola pitched forward. Right into Hamish's chest. His hands came out to steady her.

'Lola?'

'Hamish.' He smelled *so* good—coconut and pine—that for a second she just stood in the circle of his arms and breathed him in.

Too quickly, he eased her away and Lola noticed he had his keys in his hands. 'You're on your way out?'

'Yes.' His grin was really big, and that impossibly square jaw of his was looking absolutely wonderful covered in ginger scruff. 'I was coming to you.'

He kissed her then, pushing her against the open doorway, and Lola *melted*, moaning deep in the back of her throat, her hands going up around his neck to shift nearer, to bring him closer. Her head filled with the scent of him and the sound of his breathing and the taste of beer on his breath.

'Oh, I missed you,' he muttered, and his words filled her head too, making her feel dizzy.

Intoxicating her.

She was drunk. Drunk on the feel and the

taste and the smell of him. On his heat and his hardness. But…they had to talk first.

There were things he needed to hear, things she needed to say. And if they kept this up there'd be no talking. There'd be nudity in the hallway and sex on the doorstep. God knew, she wanted him badly but she had to prove to him she *could* talk with her mouth, not just her body.

Lola pulled away, placing a hand on his chest as Hamish came back in for more. Their breathing was heavy between them as his gaze searched hers. 'We need to talk.'

'Lola, I don't care.' He dropped his lips to her neck and nuzzled. 'I don't bloody care.' His words were muffled and hot on her neck and Lola's eyes felt as if they'd rolled all the way back in her head as he teased her there, his tongue and his whiskers a potent combination.

'I've held out for as long as I can and I just don't care any more. You win. Whatever kind of relationship you want, I'm in. We don't have to talk ever. I just need you too bloody much.'

His words were like a rush to her brain. And places significantly south. But they didn't give her any great satisfaction. She'd treated him like a sex object. Like a life support for a penis and that had been wrong.

'Hamish.' Lola broke away again.

He pulled back, his pupils dilated with lust, his breathing raspy. 'Come to bed with me. Let me show you how much I missed you.'

And he kissed her again, long and drugging, and she clung to him, blood pounding through her breasts and belly and surging between her thighs as the dizziness took her again. The man could definitely kiss. He sure as hell made it hard to stop.

But. This was important. It was their future.

Lola pushed hard against his chest this time and Hamish groaned as he pulled away again. 'You accused me of not wanting to talk.' She was panting but determined to see this through. 'And you were right. So I'm going to do this properly. We're going to *talk*. And then you can take me to bed and do whatever you want with me.'

He searched her gaze for a moment before breaking into a smile. 'Whatever I want?'

Lola's heart swelled with love. 'Anything.' She'd give this man anything.

He grinned. 'You're on.' Then he stepped back, grabbed her hand and urged her inside. 'Let's go to the balcony. I won't be tempted to take off your clothes out there. *Probably.*'

Lola laughed. She didn't care where they talked, only that they did, and she followed him out to the balcony with its view of the Manly foreshore in the distance. She could hear the distant noise from New Year's Eve revellers floating to her on the balmy night air.

Hamish stood at the railing, his arms folded across his chest as if he couldn't be trusted not to touch her, and Lola smiled. She settled against the railing too, leaving a few feet between them.

'Speak.'

She didn't speak. Instead, she reached into the pocket of her work trousers—because she hadn't stopped to change—and handed over May's postcard. He took it impatiently, staring at the picture. 'What's this?'

'It's a postcard from May.'

'Well, yeah, I figured that. I mean why are—?'

'I got it today. It's postmarked the twenty-first.'

He glanced at her swiftly. 'Oh, Lola.' He took a step in her direction and stopped. 'Are you okay?'

Lola nodded. 'I am, actually.'

'It's kinda freaky, yeah?'

'Yeah.' Lola smiled. 'A little.'

'Listen, I've been thinking. I could come with you…to Doongabi…keep you company.'

Hamish no doubt knew about all the funeral arrangements. She'd only responded in a perfunctory manner to his texts and hadn't answered any of his calls, but Grace was up to speed with all the details.

Lola's heart filled up a little more at Hamish's offer. 'You have to be back at work in Toowoomba.'

'I'm sure I can figure it out with my boss.'

'Well…yes, thank you. I'd like that.' She took a step towards him. There was only about a foot between them now. 'I'd like to introduce my family to the man I love.'

She could hear Hamish's breath catch and caught the blanching of his knuckles as he gripped the railing. 'The man you love?'

'Yes.' Lola nodded and her heart banged in her chest. This was it. The moment of truth. 'I love you, Hamish. I'm so sorry it took me this long to see it. That I was so blind to it, too wedded to this idea of being a gypsy, too frightened to deviate from the path I'd set myself all those years ago, to see what my heart already knew.'

'You *love* me.'

He was very still suddenly and Lola rushed to reassure him. 'Yes. *God, yes.*' Her hands were trembling and she folded her arms to quell the action. 'It took a postcard and some words from Aunty May and my heart transplant patient to realise that I've only been living a half-life and a gypsy caravan is big enough for two and I want to share mine with you.'

'You do?'

'Yes.' Stupid tears threatened and Lola blinked them back. She was done with crying. 'And I treated you like a…sex object—'

His laugh cut her off. 'Well, that bit wasn't so bad.'

Lola laughed too. 'That bit was pretty damn good. But it was wrong of me. You were *always* more than that. You were the guy who made me laugh. The guy who held me when I was sad. The guy who watched *Die Hard* with me. The guy who bought me the most beautifully perfect gift I've ever been given. I've been falling in love with you all this time and lying to myself about it because I've been single for so long I don't know how to be part of a couple.'

'Lola.' Hamish took that one last remaining step and brought his body flush with hers, his hands sliding possessively onto her hips. He smiled. 'You should stop talking now and kiss me.'

Lola shook her head, pressing a hand between them as worry that she might screw things up grew like a bogeyman inside her head. 'I mean it, Hamish, I don't know how to do this. And we're so different, we want different things. I still don't know how we're going to work it all out.'

He smiled gently. 'Do you love me, Lola?'

She nodded. 'Yes. *God, yes.*'

'Do you want to be with me? In the forever kind of way.'

'Yes,' she whispered. 'I want forever with you.'

'Good answers, *City.*' He smiled and Lola relaxed and fell in love a little more. 'All that matters is that we love each other. We can work the rest out. Sure, it'll take compromise and we'll probably argue a little and go back and forth a hundred times over the same old things but as long as we're committed to staying together, we can overcome anything. We'll be all right, Lola, I promise.'

Suddenly, Lola knew he was right. She could feel it in her bones. Because nothing was more important in her life than Hamish. And she knew he felt the same way about her.

They were going to be better than all right. They were going to be freaking amazing.

'Now.' Hamish removed her hand from his chest and urged her closer. 'Are you going to kiss me or what?'

Lola smiled, lifting on her tippytoes to kiss the man she loved, twining her arms around his neck and sighing against his mouth as their lips joined and everything in her life clicked into place.

In the distance the countdown started and they were still kissing as the crowd yelled, 'Happy New Year!'

The first firework shot into the sky with a muted *thunk* and exploded seconds later in an umbrella of red sparks. Lola and Hamish broke apart, laughing. She stared in wonder at the fireworks and at Hamish.

'I think I just saw stars.' Lola laughed up at him as the night sky erupted into a kaleidoscope of noise and colour.

He grinned. 'Me too. Now, let's go make the earth move.' And he tugged on her hand and led her to his bedroom.

EPILOGUE

A COOLING HARBOUR breeze blew cross the park on the warm November morning. Flurries of electric purple jacaranda flowers swirled and drifted to the ground, carpeting the road and the footpath and the edge of the park where the ceremony was being held in a stunning lilac carpet.

'Do you take this woman…?'

Lola's hands tightened in Hamish's as she smiled up at her soon-to-be husband and her heart did its usual *kerthump*. It had been his idea to have the marriage service here, in this place she loved so much. And, if it was possible, her heart expanded a little more.

Having Grace and Marcus joining them to make it a double wedding was the icing on the cake. They'd already said their vows and were waiting eagerly for Lola and Hamish to get through theirs so they could all be declared husbands and wives.

Grace was looking radiant in her figure-hugging cream lace creation, her gorgeous red hair piled into a classy up-do. Marcus was darkly handsome in his suit and still only had eyes for Grace.

Lola had chosen a more gypsy-style dress of embroidered cotton that flowed rather than clung. It had shoestring straps and fluttered against her body in the breeze, the garland of jacaranda flowers in her loose, curly hair the perfect finishing touch.

'I sure as hell do.'

The wedding guests—a mix of friends and both families who'd travelled to Sydney for the occasion—laughed at Hamish's emphatic answer and Lola's heart just about burst with happiness. He was breathtakingly sexy in his fancy suit with his purple shirt. His clean-shaven jaw was as rock solid as always, his reddish-brown hair flopped down over his forehead as endearingly as always and his bottomless blue gaze was full of promises to come.

It had been a whirlwind year—falling in love, getting engaged and planning a wedding in such a short space of time but, as Aunty May had said, when you knew, you *knew*.

Hamish hadn't gone back to Toowoomba, he'd stayed on in Sydney to complete his course, finishing it while Lola had been in

Zimbabwe then joining her there for the last week, taking Aunt May's ashes with him. Together they'd scattered them from a canoe across the mighty Zambezi River, a place as wild and free as May herself.

Tomorrow they were leaving for two weeks in London before heading to western Queensland. Hamish was taking up a two-year rural post and Lola had a job at the local hospital. *And* she was looking forward to it.

It had taken her very little time with Hamish to learn that home was wherever her heart was and her heart would always be with him. They'd even talked about having children when they returned to Sydney.

Children!

Lola had always assumed she'd remain childless, like May. Now she couldn't wait to be running around after a little blonde girl and little boy with cinnamon hair. She'd been a lot of places and seen a lot of things but what she craved most now was home and hearth and family.

It was official, she was a hundred percent, head-over-heels gone on Hamish Gibson.

'And do you take this man…?'

The celebrant was smiling at her. Grace was smiling at her. Her mother was smiling at her. And Hamish… Hamish was smiling at her.

'Yes,' Lola said, her eyes misting over. 'For ever and ever.'

More laughter but Hamish squeezed her hands tighter and, as the jacaranda flowers twirled around their heads in the breeze, she knew she'd never spoken truer words.

He was hers. And she was his.

For ever.

* * * * *

*If you missed the previous story in the
Nurses in the City duet, look out for*

Reunited with Her Brooding Surgeon
by Emily Forbes

*And if you enjoyed this story, check out
these other great reads from
Amy Andrews*

A Christmas Miracle
Swept Away by the Seductive Stranger
It Happened One Night Shift
200 Harley Street: The Tortured Hero

All available now!